MW01114057

THE LIFE AND TIMES
OF SHEROCK HOLMES

ESSAYS ON VICTORIAN ENGLAND
VOLUME FOUR

LIESE SHERWOOD-FABRE, PhD

LITTLE ELM PRESS, LLC

ISBN: 978-1-952408-21-2

Praise for Liese Sherwood-Fabre

Prepare to be enlightened and entertained!

— Bestselling Author, Carole Nelson Douglas

Valuable nuggets for understanding authentic Victorian life.

— Bestselling Author, Kathleen Baldwin

A gem for fans and non-fans alike.

— Amazon Reviews

To Charlotte Fabre,
The newest addition to our family

Contents

In two of Holmes' cases, he meets Pinkerton agents: Edwards in *The Valley of Fear* and Leverton, who trailed Giuseppe Gorgiano from America in "The Adventure of the Red Circle." By 1888, during the first encounter, the reputation of the Pinkerton Agency had been firmly established for almost 50 years and had already lost its founder, Allan Pinkerton. The Edwards character is said to have been based on James McFarland, who had garnered fame in the 1870s for infiltrating and testifying against the Molly Maguires, a secret Irish mining society. (1) Leverton's fame also preceded him as "the hero of the Long Island cave mystery."

Allan Pinkerton was born in Glasgow, Scotland in 1819 and worked as a barrel maker there until immigrating to the US in 1842. He settled outside of Chicago and continued his trade. In 1847, he fell into his new profession when he was out collecting materials for his barrels. A particular island not far from where he lived had a plentiful supply of poles, and while gathering them one summer day, he came across evidence of someone else using the island. He informed the sheriff, and the officer investigated, capturing a large gang of counterfeiters. Later, local shopkeepers asked Pinkerton to help capture yet another counterfeiter. Based on these efforts, he was appointed as Chicago's first—and, in the beginning, only—police detective. Shortly, he had five detectives working under him, and his reputation continued to grow. (2)

Beyond his detective work, he was also an abolitionist. He had been involved in radical politics in Scotland, which was why he was forced to emigrate. His shop served as a station along the underground railroad, (3) and he raised funds to help transport eleven slaves freed by John Brown.

In 1850 he left public services to form his agency. Pinkerton's National Detective Agency advertised "We Never Sleep" with an unblinking eye as its logo. This image lies behind the term "private eye." (4) The company included Allan's brother Robert, who was a railroad contractor. The organization specialized in the capture of counterfeiters and train robbers, but also provided private military contractors and security guards. (5) By 1853, Pinkerton Agencies existed in all the major Union cities. (6) The company hired the first female detective (Kate Warne) in 1856, (7) and during an investigation of a railway case, uncovered a plot to assassinate President-elect Abraham Lincoln in 1861. Warned of the threat, Lincoln changed his itinerary and, under a disguise, passed through the area at night unharmed. (8)

When the Civil War broke out, Lincoln brought Pinkerton to Washington to head the first national police force—a secret service division of the army. Pinkerton agents provided information regarding the Confederacy's military plans. Such feats were dramatized by William Gillette, famous for his portrayal of Sherlock Holmes, in a play he wrote and starred in as a Union spy sent south as Captain Thorne to send false information to the Confederate army, allowing Union troops to break through their lines. *Secret Service* debuted in 1896, and Gillette reprised his role as Captain Thorne almost 1800 times. (9)

When General McClellan was replaced by General Grant, Pinkerton returned to Chicago, where he focused primarily on bank robbers. (10) The agency introduced several innovations, including photographing criminals after arrest and incorporating newspaper stories about them and their crimes in their files. As a result, by the 1870s, they had the country's largest criminal database and were often consulted by local law enforcement for descriptions of possible suspects. (11) Unfortunately, most of these were destroyed during the 1871 Chicago Fire—along with their offices. The agents themselves, however, were hired to serve as guards and prevent looting in the fire's aftermath.

Following the death of Allan Pinkerton in 1884, his sons took control of the company, and businesses hired the agency to infiltrate unions to prevent strikes and factory shutdowns. Such "union busting" efforts led to a decline in the agency's reputation, which sank even lower when eleven people, including three Pinkerton agents, were killed during the Homestead Strike of 1892. (12)

Despite several highly publicized incidents (such as firebombing Jesse James' mother's home), the agency endured and has grown to a $1.5 billion organization. Its Website boasts operations in 100 countries and offers such services as security management, corporate investigations, and intelligence protection.

At the time of Holmes' adventures with these agents, the Pinkertons' reputation still netted Sherlock's respect, and had they been given a chance to review Holmes' own scrapbook collection of criminal activity, each would have found a kindred spirit in the other.

If interested in Gillette's original play Secret Service, *you can read the entire script (including stage directions) here: http://books. google.com/books?AAYAAJ&source=gbs_navlinks_s*

---

1. https://en.wikipedia.org/wiki/ James_McFarland_Valley_of_Fear: .22meets.22_Holmes
2. http://www.frvpld.info/sites/default/ files/u98/ pinkerton_13.pdf
3. http://www.americaslibrary.gov /jb/nation/jb_nation_pinkerto_1.html
4. https://www.pbs.org/wgbh/american experience/features/james-agency/

5. https://www.legendsofamerica.com/ allan-pinkerton
6. https://chroniclingamerica.loc.gov /lccn/sn83045462/1884-07-05/ed-1/seq-3/
7. https://pinkerton.com/our-story/history
8. https://www.loc.gov/item/today-in-history/august-25/
9. https://immortalephemera.com/52226 /secret-service-1931/
10. https://law.jrank.org/pages/9212/ Pinkerton-Agents.html#ixzz6ZovY3k69
11. https://law.jrank.org/pages/9212/ Pinkerton - Agents.html
12. https://www.legendsofamerica.com/ pinkertons/

A Shot in the Dark

F irearms figured prominently in three of the cases in the Canon:
the very special airgun of Colonel Sabastian Moran in "The
Adventure of the Empty House," the apparent death of Hilton
Cubitt, and his wife's suicide in "The Adventure of the Dancing
Men," and the apparent murder of Maria Gibson by one of a pair of
her husband's revolvers from his "arsenal" in "The Adventure of
Thor Bridge." In all three deaths, Holmes' knowledge of weapons
and ballistics provided the true nature and sequence of events.

Holmes was known to use several different firearms, including a
.45-caliber Webley Metropolitan Police RIC (Royal Irish Constabu-
lary) revolver, a .45-caliber British Bull Dog (a pocket revolver), and a
Webley RIC chambered in .442 (his pistol of choice). (1) Watson's
trusty service revolver was most likely a .45-caliber Adams,
purchased with his own funds, with the ammunition supplied by the
government during his service years. (2) While it could be assumed
Holmes was no slouch with his aim (he couldn't have "decorated" his
flat with the initials "VR" in bullet holes without a great deal of preci-
sion), Baring-Gould concluded Watson was the better shot. The
doctor needed only a single bullet to take down a mastiff in "The
Adventure of the Copper Beeches," while Holmes needed five to do
the same with the hound of the Baskervilles. (3)

When first developed, guns were hand-held canons where the

shooter loaded gunpowder and a steel ball into the barrel and lit a fuse. A trigger and a percussion cap later replaced the fuse. Adding a revolving chamber that held several shots reduced the need to reload and created the revolver. By the 1870s, instead of filling each chamber with gunpowder, these weapons used a bullet cartridge containing the projectile, gunpowder, and an explosive cap. Today, as then, when the shooter pulls the trigger, a hammer draws back and then springs forward to hit the cartridge and its cap. The gunpowder explodes and forces the bullet down the barrel of the gun. (4)

A gun's caliber refers to the internal diameter of the gun's barrel and is important in identifying the make of the handgun. (5) As noted above, most of Holmes' and Watson's firearms were .45 caliber, meaning the interior diameter of Watson's trusty service revolver was .45 inches. Colonel Sabastian Moran, on the other hand, deceived law enforcement by using a soft revolver bullet in his airgun.

In addition to the type of gun and bullet used in a crime, another part of forensics—referred to as "firearm examination"—involves gunshot evidence on either the victim or suspect. As noted above, when a bullet is fired, the gunpowder explodes. The gases and other particles created by this explosion follow the bullet and escape through the end as well as spaces in the weapon itself. Revolvers are particularly "holey" and leave more of this residue on the shooter. In the case of the victim, gunshot residue (GSR) can be used to determine how far the victim was from the weapon. The closer the two, the more GSR will be found. (6) Holmes used this knowledge of GSR to conclude that William Kirwan in "The Adventure of the Reigate Squire" was not shot during a struggle over a gun as reported, because his clothes carried no black marks from being shot at close range.

He also used his knowledge of GSR and ballistics in "The Adventure of the Dancing Men" to determine the presence of a third shooter in the murder of Hilton Cubitt. Ballistics is the study of how bullets (and other projectiles) travel. (7) He noted the lack of powder marks on the victim, but some on Mrs. Cubitt's hands, and a third bullet hole through a window sash, indicating a third shot and shooter. Taken together, the evidence indicated Cubitt and the third person exchanged gunshots—one with deadly aim and the second missing its intended victim. Upon finding her husband dead, Mrs. Cubitt unsuccessfully attempted to take her own life and would have been tried for murder without Holmes' keen observations and discovery of the third shot.

Holmes' knowledge of firearm investigations took a more mathematical bent in "The Adventure of Thor Bridge." One of a pair of revolvers was found in the suspect's wardrobe. The other was missing. Given that two minus one leaves one, the second revolver was the murder weapon—especially when a new chip appeared on the bridge railing where the victim died. Several criminologists and Sherlockian have noted this case resembled an 1893 suicide described by Hans Gross. In this actual event, a grain merchant staged his suicide to appear as a homicide by tying a stone to his pistol and letting it be dragged over a bridge and into the water. (8)

While firearms appeared in several of the Canon's cases, including one where a mysterious widow fired "barrel after barrel," instead of "chamber after chamber" to end the life of Charles Augustus Milverton, (9) Holmes' observations and the use of his knowledge of ballistics and related firearm traits were of particular importance in a smaller number. All the same, his conclusions were never proved to be a shot in the dark.

---

1. https://literary007.com/2015/03/31/armed-for-her-majesty-james-bond-and-sherlock-holmes-weaponry/
2. https://simanaitissays.com/2015/05/15/firearms-of-the-holmesian-canon/
3. William S. Baring-Gould, *The Annotated Sherlock Holmes, Volume II.* New York: Clarkson N Potter, Inc., 1967, page 131.

4. https://science.howstuffworks.com/revolver2.htm
5. D.P. Lyle, *Forensics for Dummies*. Hoboken, NJ: John Wiley & Sons, Inc., 2019, page 311.
6. Lyle, page 316-318.
7. Lyle, page 307.
8. https://journals.lww.com/amjforensicmedicine/Fulltext/2016/06000/Disguising_a_Suicide_as_a_Homicide__Sir_Arthur.9.aspx
9. Baring-Gould, page 569.
10. https://creativecommons.org/licenses/by-sa/2.0/deed.en

A Fine Pair of Bracelets

Handcuffs were used to detain nine persons in the Canon:

- Jefferson Hope in *A Study in Scarlet*
- Jonathan Small in *The Sign of the Four*
- John Clay in "The Adventure of the Red-Headed League" (referred to as "derbies," but pronounced "darbies")
- Abe Slaney in "The Adventure of the Dancing Men"
- Patrick Cairns in "The Adventure of Black Peter"
- Josiah Brown in "The Adventure of the Six Napoleons"
- Culverton Smith in "The Adventure of the Dying Detective"
- Count Sylvius and Sam Merton in "The Adventure of the Mazarin Stone"

Restraining prisoners, criminals, slaves, or others to deter their ability to flee or injure people most likely dates back to prehistoric times. Bindings made of hides or other material were probably the first such bonds. Once metal work developed, hand and foot shackles were designed. (1) These were most likely created even before coins, appearing in the Bronze Age and requiring a rivet to secure them. (2)

The Greeks and others used shackles to control prisoners of war. Chariots full of these devices would be brought to the battlefield in anticipation of the enemies' capture. The design involved a u-shaped piece of metal around the wrists and closed by a bar that could either be stamped shut as a more permanent device or locked to restrain someone temporarily. This "one size fits all" device created a major drawback. Prisoners with small enough hands or wrists could slip them off and escape. (3)

In the early 1800s, the most common handcuffs used in Britain were the "Bango," which resembled a double oxen yoke for the hands and did not permit any movement, and the "Flexible" (or Darby) with a link between the cuffs on each hand that allowed some movement, such as for eating. Both of these were still "one size fits all" and required some effort to place on the prisoner. (4)

The introduction of ratchets, patented by W.V. Adams in 1862, on a cuff with a "swing gate" created the first adjustable bindings to fit large and small wrists. (5) Several additional modifications to this design by John Tower included the ratchet notches on the inside of the swing gate, the placement of the lock case on the side of the frame, and a release button to keep the cuffs from locking until applied to the prisoner's wrist. (6)

Such restraints, however, could be shimmied by sliding a piece of metal between the two sides of the cuff. They were also difficult to lock because the key had to be turned several times. These draw-backs, however, were addressed in 1912 by George Carney. The device he patented resembled those used today: a lightweight, swing-thru gate design that could be secured without a key. Easily slapped onto a person's wrist, a policeman only needed one hand to quickly restrain a criminal. (7)

The major parts of a handcuff include:

- **The single strand,** the moving part that loosens or tightens the cuff
- **The teeth** or ratchet at the end of the single strand to hold it in place after passing into
- **The double strand** or gap that holds the single strand in place by
- **The pawl**, which is spring-loaded and must be moved up to allow the single strand to pass into the double strand. This is accomplished by inserting a key into
- **The keyway**
- **A rivet** connects the single strand to the double strand and is what allows the cuff to adjust around the wrist
- **A link** attaches the two cuffs and allows limited movement

In three cases in the Canon, handcuffs are referred to as "bracelets," and interestingly, women wore gold bracelets that resembled handcuffs in the late Victorian era. These were often presented by a gentleman to a young woman in place of an engagement ring to indicate the woman was now "bound" to her future husband. (8) Whether criminal or future bride, either might be told they "had a fine pair of bracelets."

For images of British and other handcuffs, check out this site: http://www.handcuffs.org/g/index.php?mode=1

---

1. https://unitedlocksmith.net/blog/the-history-of-handcuffs
2. http://torturemuseum.net/en/the-stand-of-shackles/
3. https://unitedlocksmith.net/blog/the-history-of-handcuffs
4. https://www.blueline.ca/a_history_of_ handcuffs-2396/

5. http://lawenforcementservices.biz/law_
enforcement_services,_llc/ Antique_
Handcuffs_files/A%20Brief%20
History%20of%20US%20Handcuffs.pdf
6. https://www.encyclopedia.com/manufacturing/news-
wires-white-papers-and-books/ handcuffs
7. http://lawenforcementservices.biz/law_
enforcement_services,_llc/ Antique_ Handcuffs_files/
A%20Brief%20 History%20of%20US%20
Handcuffs.pdf
8. https://www.mimimatthews.-
com/2017/10/02/victorian- handcuff-bracelets-for-
engagement-and-marriage/

Got You Under My Skin

In "The Adventure of the Red-Headed League," a fish tattoo above the right wrist of Jabez Wilson told Sherlock Holmes his guest had been to China. Holmes's study and writings on tattoos indicated Wilson's inking could only have been done in that country.

The practice of tattooing can be found in cultures all over the world from very ancient times. Implements for marking the skin, dating back more than 12,000 years, have been found in France, Portugal, and Scandinavia. (1) Ötzi, the "Iceman" discovered in 1991 on the Italian-Austrian border, displays the oldest actual markings. His remains were carbon-dated back 5200 years. (2)

Tattoos, however, were not limited to European countries. They have been found in ancient Egypt (but only on women), the Scythian Pazyryk in the Altai Mountains, ancient Briton, ancient Greece and Rome, pre-Columbian civilizations of Peru and Chile, the Cree, China, Japan, and the Polynesian cultures. This last group, which James Cook visited in Tahiti in 1769, provided the contemporary name to such marks. Their term "tatatau" or "tattau" became "tattoo." (3)

Ötzi sported about fifty lines and crosses marked on various parts of his body, including his spine, knee and ankle joints. Interestingly, these are also the points used in traditional Chinese acupuncture, although the earliest indications of the use of needles on pressure points didn't occur for another 2000 years. Researchers believe these tattoos were used for therapeutic purposes related to arthritis and abdominal pain. (4) Similar uses were found in female Egyptian mummies where tattoos were believed to be related to childbirth. (5)

Tattoos served additional purposes over the centuries. The Romans and Japanese marked criminals. Slaves carried an indication of ownership. North and South American cultures as well as Britons used them for ceremonial purposes. Scandinavians and Saxons carried a family crest. Europeans who joined the crusades often had a cross on their hand to indicate a desire for a Christian burial. Sailors and miners had them for identification in case of a disaster. (6)

Various methods have been used to create tattoos, but all require a means of puncturing the second layer of skin, or dermis, to apply a pigment underneath. This skin layer isn't shed like the epidermis, and the pigmentation becomes permanent. The implement to puncture the skin requires a sharp point—today a needle—that will penetrate to this layer. (7) Current electric tattoo machines use the same basic model as that patented in 1891, based on Thomas Edison's electric engraver pen. Pigmentations have included soot, cinnabar (for red markings), and cadmium compounds for hues such as orange and yellow. (8) The pigments used in modern tattoos are from colorless metal salts that give off different hues when light refracts off them. (9)

As Sherlock noted concerning Jabez Wilson's tattoo, different tattoo artists use different types of pigments as well as each having their own style. Modern-day forensic experts are able to extract some of the pigment, which investigators use to exclude or confirm a particular artist's work. (10) Michelle Miranda, author of *Forensic Analysis of Tattoos and Tattoo Inks*, described the chemical analysis of the tattoo pigments as assisting in determining "the age, quality or prevalence of the ink." Ancient pigments were carbon-based, but by the late 1800s, ink colors were introduced (mostly black, blue, green, and red). From the mid- to late-1900s, the pigments contained high concentrations of heavy metals. Currently, most of the colors are synthetic organic, and the designs have finer lines with more and brighter colors. (11)

Tattoos fell out of favor in Europe with the spread of Christianity. These markings were considered a disfigurement of those "made in God's image," with Emperor Constantine going so far as banning them in the fourth century. Certain populations—such as sailors and miners, mentioned above—continued the practice even in the Victorian era. (12) Currently, about one in seven people in North America sport at least one tattoo. (13) Some of this increased popularity among the general public has been attributed to the TV show "Miami Ink," which premiered in 2005 and showcased the artistry involved in such work. (14)

Watson didn't document much about Holmes' investigation into the practice of tattooing. As he displayed in "The Adventure of the Red-Headed League," however, his treatises on the subject were bound to have included extensive information on the types of inks, craftmanship, and symbols—all going more than just skin deep.

1. https://interestingengineering.com/the-very-long-and-fascinating-history- of-tattoos
2. https://www.smithsonianmag.com/ history/ tattoos-144038580/
3. https://www.smithsonianmag.com/ history/ tattoos-144038580/
4. https://www.mcgill.ca/oss/article/ history- you-asked/ what- history- tattoos
5. https://www.smithsonianmag.com/ history/ tattoos-144038580/
6. https://www.mcgill.ca/oss/article/ history- you-asked/what- history-tattoos
7. https://interestingengineering.com/the-very-long-and-fascinating- history-of-tattoos

8. https://inchemistry.acs.org/atomic-news/tattoo-ink.html#:~:text=Historically%2C%20pigments%20used%20in%20tattoo,used%20to%20produce%20red%20hues.
9. https://www.mcgill.ca/oss/article/ history- you-asked/what- history-tattoos
10. D.P. Lyle, *Forensics for Dummies*. Hoboken, NJ: John Wiley and Sons, Inc., 2019, page 160.
11. https://www.the4thwall.net/blog/2017/2 /8/inkspector
12. https://www.smithsonianmag.com/ history/tattoos-144038580/
13. https://www.mcgill.ca/oss/article history- you-asked/what- history- tattoos
14. https://www.huffpost.com/entry/how- tattoos-went-from-sub_b_6053588

Did You Hear...?

S herlock Holmes was not above acquiring and using gossip for his own purposes. In "The Adventure of Wisteria Lodge," he spent time among the village gossips to collect information on Mr. Henderson of High Gable, collected similar information from the publican in "The Adventure of the Solitary Cyclist," and consulted with Langdale Pike, a gossip merchant, in "The Adventure of the Three Gables." While gossip is often viewed negatively, beyond helping to solve cases, it is an important part of social interaction.

Researchers distinguish between rumors and gossip. Rumors are "public communications that are infused with private hypotheses about how the world works," which help individuals (and societies) to make sense of what is occurring and assist in coping with anxieties and uncertainties. These may involve hoped-for consequences (wish rumors) or feared consequences (dread rumors) and often spread faster when anxieties are intense. (1) Holmes confronted such a situation in the investigation of the death of Sir Charles Baskerville, where villagers attributed the man's death to the superstition surrounding a hound and a curse on his family. Although in this case, the rumor was not without merit.

Gossip, on the other hand, encompasses a major portion of human interaction. While associated with sharing negative information about others, scientists define gossip as "talking about people who aren't present," which can be positive, negative, or neutral.

17

Studies have found that such talk breaks down into 76% neutral, 15% negative, and 9% positive, and theories suggest that these conversations are what helped early man survive. (2)

Such models suggest language developed to build social networks. The basis of this and similar hypotheses is that language is a social behavior, sharing information on who did what among the network's members. (3) While such communications might be viewed as "idle chit-chat," a study conducted in India found using a village's recognized "gossips" (identified by others in the community) was an effective means of diffusing important public health information and increasing others' positive actions. (4)

In addition to providing useful information, gossip has also been found to be an effective means of moderating social behavior. In one study, participants played a game in which monetary rewards were divided at the end of each round of play. Over the course of several games, players shared information about participants who kept more of their winnings for themselves. The others ostracized such stingy players and actually forced them to be more cooperative and generous than in earlier games. (5)

When gossip involves a severe enough transgression—one involving a social norm that will result in the general public's rejection of the transgressor—it plays a role in creating a scandal through publicizing the behavior. Such information sharing can be both by word of mouth as well as through other media—those papers that specialized in such information that Langdale Pike supplied as well as social media of today. (6) In several cases in the Canon, perpetrators committed a crime to prevent the spread of such information and, thus, avoid a scandal. The ostracism that could have ensued from such common knowledge of their action might have led to the destruction of their livelihood, marriage, or social status. In more than one case, Holmes chose to assist them in averting such gossip by applying his own concept of justice, and rather than sharing it with the legal authorities, kept the particulars to himself.

As Watson noted, many of his case notes in the dispatch box at

Cox & Co. held others' secrets—most likely enough to raise Langdale Pike's income even higher. Luckily for such clients, Holmes respected their confidences.

---

1. https://www.apa.org/science/about/psa/2005/04/gossip
2. https://time.com/5680457/why-do-people-gossip/
3. https://www.psychologytoday.com/us/ blog/ talking-apes/201502/why-you-were-born-gossip
4. https://academic.oup.com/restud/article / 86/6/2453/5345571
5. https://www.apa.org/science/about/psa/2005/04/gossip
6. Ari Adut, *On Scandal: Moral Disturbances in Society, Politics and Art,* Cambridge: Cambridge University Press, 2008.

Just Can It

Holmes was not above putting convenience over luxury in certain circumstances. In *The Hound of the Baskervilles*, he camped out on the moors in an ancient dwelling, subsisting on tinned foods such as tongue and peaches. Over the 19th century, tinning—or canning—foodstuffs provided an important means of increasing the variety and quality of people's diets.

For centuries, humans sought methods of preserving foods to make it through lean times—either long winters, droughts, or when on the move. Smoking, salting, pickling, and drying foods developed over the centuries. Such methods, however, had their drawbacks, and in 1795, the French government, seeking a means of sustaining their soldiers and sailors across the empire offered a prize for the development of an effective and efficient means of food preservation. The winner, Nicolas Appert, created a means of packing food—along with a mixture of cheese and lime—in airtight champagne bottles. Over time, the bottles evolved into wide-necked glass containers, and the French navy sent out the vegetables, fruit, meat, dairy, and fish on a sea trial in 1803. Appert published his method in 1810, and soon others were preserving various foods across the world. (1)

Glass containers, however, tended to explode, and another Frenchman, Philippe de Girard developed a method of using tin cans in 1811. (2) A British merchant, Bryan Donkin, purchased the patent for tinned foods and produced these on a large scale to supply the Royal Navy and arctic explorers. Such foodstuffs, however, were not without their dangers. The 1845 British arctic expedition saw the death of several crew members from lead poisoning. The bodies of the first three to perish were exhumed in 1984. An examination of different tissues from these well-preserved men indicated acute lead poisoning. Tests of some of the remaining tins revealed some of the cans' seams had not been correctly sealed and led to contamination of much of the supply. Researchers speculate that these errors occurred because the order for the expedition was rushed through production without proper quality control. (3)

Canning was introduced in the US in 1825 with the introduction of canned oysters, fruits, meats, and vegetables, but it was Bordon's condensed milk that made the process a commercial success. (4) Gail Borden introduced his Eagle Brand sweetened condensed milk in 1856 and became an important military supplier during the Civil War. The product was also credited with reducing infant mortality in North America because it remained safe until use. (5)

Cans and tins, however, predated any type of means of opening them by about fifty years. Tops had to be chiseled or pried open with an implement such as a hammer or bayonet. (6) The can opener finally came along in 1858 when Ezra Warner patented his device. The instrument included a bar with a pointed tip used to pierce the can. A sickle-shaped cutter was inserted into the piercing and sawed around the can to open it. It was very popular among soldiers during the Civil War but was considered too dangerous for domestic use. Grocers kept one on hand to open cans for their customers before they left the store. (7)

While Appert developed a method for preserving food, the science behind his process was not provided until 1865 when Louis Pasteur patented his process for heating wine to destroy micro-organisms. (8) Following this development, Samuel Prescott and William Underwood provided a scientifically-based time and temperature table to ensure canned foods were sterilized and safe for future consumption. (9) Different foods require different amounts of time at

240-250°F (depending on the content's acidity, density, and ability to transfer heat) to ensure their safety for two years or more. (10)

Today, most foods are packed near the source and often at the peak of harvest. As a result, few nutrients are lost during the process and can sometimes even be enhanced. Today, any food that is grown can be canned. (11) Quite a long way from tinned tongue and peaches.

1. https://www.history.com/news/what-it-says-on-the-tin-a-brief-history-of-canned-food
2. https://www.foodingredientfacts.org/apperttotheballbrothers/
3. https://www.historytoday.com/archive/ canned-food-sealed-icemens-fate
4. https://www.foodingredientfacts.org/apperttotheballbrothers/
5. https://www.eaglebrand.com/history
6. https://www.history.com/news/what-it-says-on-the-tin-a-brief-history-of-canned-food
7. http://www.patentlyinteresting.com/january-5.html
8. https://www.sciencehistory.org/historical-profile/louis-pasteur
9. https://www.britannica.com/topic/canning-food-processing
10. http://www.foodreference.com/html/artcanninghistory.html
11. Ibid

The Fine Art of Collecting

Anumber of collectors and collections appear in the Canon. Among them are Jack Stapleton from *The Hound of the Baskervilles*, known for his butterfly and moth collection; Colonel Barclay had a weapons collection in "The Adventure of the Crooked Man;" and Baron Adelbert Gruner's tastes ran to women and Chinese pottery in "The Adventure of the Illustrious Client." Holmes and Watson are not above their own collections. Holmes has scrapbooks where he catalogs items, such as biographical information, and Watson, notes and objects from their various cases.

While the interest and art of collecting can be traced back to ancient times (Caesar referred to a "collection" as a gathering of things, and Aristotle had a herbarium), the hobby truly gained momentum in the Middle Ages and is considered an important characteristic of human society. (1) Assembling and organizing objects, such as from various cultures and societies, offer a different context for the items as they are grouped in ways not seen in nature and provide new insights into their character. (2)

The reasons behind collecting vary, but pleasure provides the basis for the desire. Finding, obtaining, and reviewing one's collection feed into the pleasure center. Acquiring a rare piece can produce pride in the owner and admiration from fellow collectors. Others enjoy the thrill of the chase and attaining one's goal. When the objects are antiques, the collection can provide the person with a sense of history, or an intellectual satisfaction. (3)

Collecting became a major interest for the nobility and landed gentry during the 1700s and 1800s. These aristocratic collectors traveled far and wide to obtain different objects (based on their interests) —art, books, animal specimens, etc.—and stored them in their "cabinets of curiosities." Such rooms, designed for keeping them safe as well as permitting private viewing, served to indicate the nobleman's power and wealth. (4) Among the most famous during this period was Stephen W. Bushnell, a Victorian authority on Chinese porcelain. He collected pieces while serving as a physician in Peking (Beijing) and later produced a number of books on the subject, increasing the interest of such works in the West. (5) No doubt some of Watson's cramming on Chinese pottery before meeting with Baron Gruner included Bushnell's research.

Perhaps the epitome of such a hobbyist in the Canon would be Nathan Garrideb, who housed his collection in a room that appeared "like a small museum," and dreamed of being a second "Hans Sloane." An eighteenth-century physician, Sir Hans Sloane began collecting while serving as the Jamaican governor's physician. While in that colony, he assembled more than 800 plants (along with specimens of animals and other curiosities) that served as the basis for his natural history work on the flora and fauna of the British Caribbean colonies. He continued to collect items from travelers after he returned to Britain, as well as absorbing other collectors' inventories. In 1753, he willed his collection to the Crown, with the condition that it be housed in a public museum. Parliament responded by creating the British Museum, using his collection as its base. (6)

As Nathan Garrideb illustrates, however, collecting can have drawbacks. Watson describes the man as "round-backed" and "cadaverous" because he never exercises and prefers to spend his time admiring his collection. While not enough information exists on the man's habits to determine whether his collecting has moved into the mental disorder of "hoarding," his behavior does suggest a pattern in that direction. (7)

Of course, Sherlock has his own hoarding tendencies, mostly related to the newspapers he carefully catalogs at some point after filling every corner with them, but just as important is Watson's, who pulled from them the sixty cases that make up the Canon. For both men, their habits did not hinder their abilities to serve as a team to solve the most intriguing of cases, but instead enhanced them.

---

1. https://lignup.com/collectibles/103-history.html
2. https://historyjournal.org.uk/2021/01/27/collecting-contexts-why-do-we-collect/
3. https://coinweek.com/education/want-stuff-eight-views-psychology-collecting/
4. https://nationalpsychologist.com/2007/01/the-psychology-of-collecting/10904.html
5. https://www.hcplive.com/view/the-psychology-of-collecting
6. https://www.britishmuseum.org/about-us/british-museum-story/sir-hans-sloane
7. Monica Schmidt, "You Have Been on eBay, I Perceive: the Psychopathology of Sherlockian Hoarding," *Baker Street Journal*, Volume 69, No. 1 (Spring 2019), pp 26-30.

Lend Me Your Ear

I n "The Adventure of the Cardboard Box," Holmes tells Watson, "[T]here is no part of the body which varies so much as the human ear." At the same time, after an examination of the ears sent to Susan Cushing, he discovered one corresponded "exactly" to that of their recipient. While not as well-known or used as fingerprints, ear prints have been used to establish a suspect's presence at a crime scene because they are unique to the individual, despite the Cushing sisters' exact match in Holmes' observation.

The pinna, or auricle, is the visible part of the ear and includes the following parts that vary from person to person (1):

- The Helix—the upper curved area
- Darwin's Tubercle—a thickening of the helix where the auricle's upper and middle thirds meet in a portion of the population, noted by Darwin as inherited from primate ancestors
- The Antihelix—the curved cartilage ridge that runs parallel to the helix within the ear and divides into
- The Triangular Fossa—an indentation near the head created by the two legs of the antihelix

- The Superior crus of the antihelix
- The Inferior crus of the antihelix
- The Scapha—the depression between the helix and the antihelix
- The Crux of the Helix—the upper ridge of cartilage surrounding the entrance to the inner ear
- The Incisura Intertragica—the indentation formed by:
- The Tragus—the cartilage protruding from the head in front of the inner ear
- The Antitragus—the protrusion at the end of the antihelix
- The Lobule, or Earlobe—the cartilage-free end of the ear. This portion of the ear may be attached or unattached to the head.

Certain characteristics of the pinna are inherited. For example, approximately forty-nine genes affect whether earlobes are attached or unattached. (2) Prominent, or protruding, ears, which occur due to a lack of cartilage or malformed cartilage, are also inherited. (3) Additional research has confirmed the following generalizations about ear shape: men's ears are larger, ears continue to grow in length and width as we age, the left and right ears tend to be symmetrical, and the overall size of ears varies according to ethnic groups. (4)

Holmes, of course, was interested in the shape of the three Cushing sisters' ears, and his observation they were all the same does not hold up under research. A study of the ears of more than 400 subjects from three generations found similarities were never 100%. Even the one set of twins in the study did not have exact-matching ears, although they had more similarities than any other siblings. A comparison of grandparents' and grandchildren's ears was found to match the least, and the non-twin siblings had more similar traits than any other pairings, but still showed enough variation to identify a single individual. (5)

The uniqueness of ear prints has been equated with those of

fingerprints—only changing less over time. Ears produce fat and wax secretions that leave behind a print when pressed to a surface, just as oils and dirt leave prints from fingers. Such impressions, usually found where a person presses his/her ear on a window or door to check for sounds, have been used since the 1950s to link a suspect to a crime. (6) The first case of a murder conviction using ear prints occurred in England in 1998. (7)

Ear individuality does not end with external structure. Each person's ear processes quiet sounds differently. While not audible to the human ear, the microscopic cells in the inner ear's cochlea vibrate, producing a noise detectable with sensitive microphones. These "otoacoustic emissions" are unique to the individual. NEC has already developed a microphone that can identify individuals from these sounds with 99% accuracy. (8)

Holmes' scrutiny of one of the severed ears and that of the eldest Cushing sister indicated the fate of the youngest. While they might not have been duplicates, current research suggests they would have been similar enough to indicate a close relationship between Susan Cushing and the victim. Almost one hundred years would pass before such an observation was scientifically verified. Holmes had, once again, anticipated later forensic science.

---

1. https://www.earwellcenters.com/ congenital-ear-deformity-microtia- and-anotia/
2. https://www.nature.com/articles/ d41586-017-07792-7
3. https://patient.info/doctor/prominent-ears
4. K. Skaria Alexander et al, "A morphometric study of the human ear," *Journal of Plastic, Reconstructive, and Aesthetic Surgery*, 2011: 64, pages 41-47.
5. Ruma Purkait, "Application of External Ear in Personal Identification: A Somatoscopic Study in Families," *Annals of Forensic Research and Analysis*, May, 2015.

6. Nitin Kausal and Purnima Kausal: Human Earprints: a Review in *Journal of Biometrics and Biostatistics*, 2011, 2:129.
7. https://hearinghealthfoundation.org/blogs/ ears-the-new-fingerprints
8. https://www.bbc.com/future/article/ 20170109-the-seven-ways-you-are-totally-unique

Taking Stock

S tock brokerage firms are mentioned in two different cases in the Canon. In addition to "The Adventure of the Stockbroker's Clerk," James Dodd in "The Adventure of the Blanched Soldier" worked as a stockbroker on Throgmorton Street. While stockbroking has existed for almost a thousand years, such firms did not become prominent in England until the 1800s.

The role of the English stockbroker and the place where they operated—the "exchange"—evolved over time. The first organized system began in France in the eleventh century as a means of regulating the buying and selling of agricultural debt. In the 1300s, commodity traders set up houses in major cities such as Amsterdam. (1) Traditionally, companies were owned by individuals or a small group. As business ventures grew larger, however, they proved to be riskier as well as requiring greater funds. Discovery voyages, overseas trading, and financing foreign military campaigns offered stock to a large number of investors who then left its management in the hands of the small group who originated the venture. The Dutch East India Company became the first such publicly traded company in 1602. (2)

In England, joint stock companies were formed in the 1500s, but the sale of shares in such enterprises was limited and did not require a stockbroker. In the late 1600s, changes in banking regulations increased the number of joint stock companies tenfold in only six years, and the first stockbrokers—who bought and sold shares as an adjunct to another profession—appeared at that time. Business was first conducted at the Royal Exchange, where other merchants also conducted business, but as the number of stockbrokers grew and displayed rowdy behavior not acceptable to others in the marketplace, the government sought to regulate them. Rather than accept such interference, these men left to set up shop in the coffee-houses between Cornhill and Lombard streets—with one of the most prominent being Jonathan's Coffeehouse on Exchange Alley. (3)

While most brokers in these exchanges were reputable, some followed less-than-acceptable practices. To have greater control over who they allowed into the exchange, some brokers left Jonathan's and set up a new exchange—called "New Jonathan's" or "The Stock Exchange." Transactions were still not regulated and any broker who could pay the daily entry fee could conduct business. (4) Two specialists arose during this time—brokers and jobbers. Brokers represented clients or investors who desired to buy or sell a particular security within a certain price range. The broker's counterpart, the jobber, offered to buy or sell the desired security to the broker (but never directly to an investor). The broker worked on a commission charged to the client while the jobber made his on the "spread" between the bid and asked-for price (the notion of "buy low, sell high"). (5)

Tension developed between the owners of the new coffeehouse and the brokers. Those running the coffeehouse preferred allowing in more patrons because of the fee charged, while the brokers were concerned about still dealing with their less reputable colleagues. In 1801, the brokers left again for a new establishment governed by written regulations for conducting business, and the modern London Stock Exchange (LSE) was created. (6)

While the LSE was the United Kingdom's most important, the Industrial Revolution brought about several new companies as well as infrastructure projects that required large capital investments, prompting the creation of about twenty stock exchanges throughout the UK. (7)

New technologies were added to link both the English and international exchanges. In 1840, the telegraph provided trade information from the New York exchange in only 20 minutes (vs. sixteen days by mail). The ticker tape replaced the telegraph in 1872, and the telephone replaced it in 1880. (8)

"The Adventure of the Stockbroker's Clerk" provided an example of the variety of investments available. Beddington stole both American railway bonds as well as mining and other company scrip from the firm Mawson and Williams. Bonds are legal evidence of the provision of long-term debt (the holder to receive reimbursement plus interest when the loan was repaid). Scrip, on the other hand, indicated ownership of a portion (share) of a company. (9) As this theft indicated, stockbroker dealings could involve hundreds of thousands of pounds, but risk was involved. Hall Pycroft lost his position with Coxon and Woodhouse when they folded after a bad investment. Thanks to a quick-thinking police officer and Holmes' assistance to the stockbroker's clerk in apprehending the culprits in this case, however, Mawson and Williams failed to suffer similar losses and disgrace.

1. https://www.theclassroom.com/the-history-of-stock-brokerage-firms-13635698.html
2. https://www.encyclopedia.com/books/ politics-and-business-magazines/london-stock-exchange-limited
3. Edward Stringham, "The Emergence of the London Stock Exchange as a Self-Policing Club," *Journal of Private Enterprise,* January, 2002.
4. https://www.londonstockexchange.com/discover/lseg/our-history
5. https://hsc.co.in/difference-between-jobber-and-broker/

6. Ranald Michie, *The London Stock Exchange: A History.* Oxford: Oxford University Press, 1999.
7. https://www.encyclopedia.com/books/politics-and-business-magazines/london-stock-exchange-limited
8. https://www.londonstockexchange.com/discover/lseg/our-history
9. https://wikidiff.com/bond/scrip

D r. Watson tried to amuse himself while waiting for Holmes' return in "The Boscombe Valley Mystery" by reading a yellow-back novel, and Violet Hunter read one to her employer Rucastle in "The Adventure of the Copper Beeches." The creation and popularity of these novels coincided with increased railway travel and represented a highly popular innovation in British publishing that, though short-lived, provided a more literate population with classics as well as original works. The public had access to Jane Austen's novels and the first British translation of Pushkin's *The Queen of Spades*, among others. (1) For current historians, they provide a glimpse into the interests and lives of Victorians. (2)

The term "yellow back" comes from an advancement in engraving developed by Edmund Evans. The wood engraver developed a process in 1847 using three printings—one with the outline and two additional blocks providing color tint. In addition, he printed these on yellow-glazed paper to give books an eye-catching cover. While paperbacks were cheaper (12.5 pence, or 25 cents vs. 25 pence or 50 cents), they were worth the added expense. The fiberboard was sturdier, and the type had been reset, making the text easier to read. (3)

While several publishers produced these books, George Rout-ledge was the most successful with his "Railway Library" series, offered from 1848 to 1899. Most of these would have been sold by William Henry Smith (W.H. Smith) from his railway bookstalls. Smith opened his first kiosk in the Euston station in 1848, and by 1860, he had stores on all major and many secondary lines. (4) Both the books and the stalls were designed to appeal to the railway trav-eler, providing light entertainment for the trip, at the end of which the book might be traded for another, thrown away, or passed on. (5) The covers, with their bright colors and action scenes, were designed to be seen from 20 yards away. (6) Given that Watson visited the railway station before starting his yellow-backed novel, he most likely picked it up at that time.

The popularity of these books was also due to their subject matter. Academic circles referred to these as "sensation" novels with stories attracting an audience through tales depicting lives of moral ambiguity: fallen women, extramarital sex, and murder. (7) Some theories also suggest that railway travel itself supported the popu-larity of such themes. Going long distances among strangers gave passengers more freedom in their reading choices without condemna-tion from family and friends. (8)

Whatever lay behind their popularity, critics became concerned about the influence these books had upon the population. W.H. Smith personally reviewed the books and their advertisements to ensure they were not morally corrupt. (9) While mainly fiction books, other topics were also offered, including science, medicine, and sports. (10) Despite such efforts, the books had their critics. Oscar Wilde in *Dorian Gray* had his depraved main character use some of these novels as a guide for his life, although in the end, he decided such corruption came from within and not through the reading mate-rial. (11)

Given the disposable nature of these books, not many exist today, although WH Smith did reproduce some for their 225th anniversary in 2017, including *The Adventures of Sherlock Holmes*. (12) Outside of the "classics," many were never published except in this format, and in an effort to preserve them for social historians and others, some projects have digitized them for future readers. Emory University has more than 1000 available for download, which can be found here: https://tinyurl.com/yjwu43hm.

While Watson found the plot in his own yellow back thin, readers of Sherlock's yellow-back adventures wouldn't have found the same.

1. https://www.hermitagebooks.com/ yellowbacks.html
2. http://shared.web.emory.edu/emory/ news /releases/2010/05/ download-19th-century-books-from-emory-libraries-web-site.html#.YOmnwhNKhhE:
3. Ibid
4. https://www.historytoday.com/archive/ first-wh-smith-railway-bookstall
5. https://victorianlondonunderworld. wordpress.com/ 2013/05/22/ fancy-a-literary tryst-the-sordid-tale-of-yellow-back-books/
6. https://blog.railwaymuseum. org.uk / yellow back-sensational-stories-railways/
7. https://victorianlondonunderworld. wordpress.com/2013/05/22/ fancy-a-literary-tryst-the-sordid-tale-of-yellow-back-books/
8. https://blog.railwaymuseum.org.uk/ yellowback-sensational-stories-railways/
9. https://blog.whsmith.co.uk/ yellowbacks-how-whsmith-brought-reading-to-the-masses/
10. http://shared.web.emory.edu/emory/ news/releases/2010/05/download-19th-century-books-from-emory-libraries-web-site.html#.YOmnwhNKhhE

11. https://victorianlondonunderworld.
    wordpress.com/2013/05/22/fancy-a-literary- tryst-the-
    sordid-tale-of-yellow-back-books/
12. https://blog.whsmith.co.uk/ yellowbacks-how-whsmith-
    brought-reading-to-the-masses/

The Truth About Opium Dens

Opium is mentioned in six cases in the Canon: in a list of Holmes' knowledge of poisons in *A Study in Scarlet*; a reference to its use among Indian rebels in *The Sign of the Four*; its use as a sedative in "Silver Blaze," "The Adventure of Wisteria Lodge," and "The Adventure of the Lion's Mane;" and once as an addictive substance in "The Man with the Twisted Lip." These references reflect the substance's varied and pervasive uses in Victorian England. Class and racial bias regarding the drug's administration and practices finally led to its re-classification as a dangerous narcotic following WWI.

The first known references to opium occurred more than five thousand years ago. The Sumerians are recognized as the first cultivators and users of the "joy plant." The practice then passed to the Assyrians and the Babylonians before it spread to the Egyptians. More than 3000 years ago, the drug entered Europe. It disappeared from the continent during the Holy Inquisition (from the 1300s to 1500s), only to be re-established by the Portuguese. Thanks to Alexander the Great, opium made it to Persia and India, and Portuguese merchants carried the practice of smoking opium to China in the 1600s. Following the spread of recreational opium use in that country, the British East India Company established a monopoly on the import of Indian opium to China in the 1700s, and expanded the trade in the 1800s following the defeat of the Chinese in two "Opium Wars." (1)

When the drug was re-introduced to Europe, it was fashioned into pills or mixed with other substances and sold as remedies for a variety of ailments for all ages (from babies to the elderly). By the 1800s, Victorians could purchase opium-based products not only from a chemist, but also barbers, tobacconists, stationers, and even wine merchants. (2) The most popular form was laudanum, a tincture of 10% opium mixed with alcohol and herbs. Sometimes referred to as the "aspirin of the nineteenth century," consumers could buy twenty to twenty-five drops for a penny, making it very affordable. While some effort was made to restrict laudanum's availability to chemist shops with the passage of the 1868 Pharmacy Act, no reduction in sales occurred because chemists were not limited in the amount sold. (3)

Class distinctions, however, separated the image of the drug and its use. Among the working class, it was viewed as a stimulant and a replacement for drink. For upper- and middle-class families, laudanum use might be a habit, but was not considered addictive. The pervasive use of the drug, however, was related as much to self-medication among the middle-class as any recreational use by the lower classes. (4)

While medicinal use was considered acceptable (even though many users showed signs of addiction), those in the lower classes, and especially those from Asia, who smoked opium were viewed in a much different light. Chinese sailors who settled in the Limehouse area introduced the practice, but their numbers were small (less than 600 permanently living in London in 1891 and representing only about 10% of all sailors coming ashore). While popular culture described the places where recreational smoking occurred—the famed "opium dens"—as dark and dangerous spaces, contemporary researchers indicate very few of these "dens" actually existed and were usually one room attached to another business. (5)

The description of such a den provided in the Holmes tale represents the image perpetuated by several writers, including Thomas De Quincey (*Confessions of an Opium Eater*), Oscar Wilde (*The Picture of Dorian Gray*), and Charles Dickens (*The Mystery of Edwin Drood*). Similarly, missionaries in China provided a comparable portrayal of such dens in that country. (6) The depiction of these places as decadent and associated with the criminal underworld directly led to an increase in racism against Asians in England and elsewhere. (7)

A variety of forces came together in the early 1900s to create a shift in attitudes toward opiates. Various medical groups and the press reported on overdose deaths and the growing number of middle-class addicts and reframed the issue as a matter of public health. Additional concern that working-class users and foreigners were corrupting the middle class led to further restrictions on opiate use. (8) With the advent of WWI, public alarm over soldiers' addictions to opiates and other drugs created an emergency, and for the first time, strict regulations were introduced to control such substances, particularly those smuggled in from the Far East. The Dangerous Drug Act of 1920 made these controls permanent and reflected shifts in attitudes regarding both the drug and the user. (9)

By the time Watson goes to the opium den in search of Isa Whitney, the good doctor recognized his patient's habit as an addiction. It was another fifteen years, however, before any governmental regulations recognized it as well.

---

1. https://www.pbs.org/wgbh/pages/frontline/shows/heroin/etc/history.html
2. https://www.bl.uk/romantics-and-victorians/articles/representations-of-drugs-in-19th-century-literature
3. https://www.historic-uk.com/HistoryUK/HistoryofBritain/ Opium-in-Victorian-Britain/
4. Virginia Berridge, "Victorian Opium Eating: Responses to Opiate Use in Nineteenth-Century England,"

Victorian Studies, Vol. 21, No. 4 (Summer, 1978), page 447.

5. https://etheses.whiterose.ac.uk/11176/1/thesisfinal.pdf

6. Xavier Paulès, "High-class opium houses in Canton during the 1930s," *Journal of the Royal Asiatic Society, Hong Kong Branch, Vol. 45 (2005), page 145.*

7. https://www.bl.uk/romantics-and-victorians/articles/representations-of-drugs-in-19th-century-literature

8. https://daily.jstor.org/how-opium-use-became-a-moral-issue/

9. Berridge, "Victorian Opium Eating," page 461.

A HANDY HELPER

A lthough handkerchiefs might appear to have a limited (and outdated) use in contemporary culture, they served a variety of purposes from their earliest appearances, several of which are illustrated throughout the Canon. The first mention occurred in *A Study in Scarlet*, when Jefferson Hope remarked that poisoning Enoch Drebber was preferable to "firing over a handkerchief" (a duel). Handkerchiefs were never mentioned in the Canon as being used to clean one's nose, but several other uses were included: wiping away tears (*The Sign of the Four*) and sweat ("The Adventure of the Beryl Coronet," "The Adventure of Wisteria Lodge," and "The Adventure of the Devil's Foot); as a gag ("The Adventure of the Solitary Cyclist" and "The Adventure of Abbey Grange"); and to bind a wound ("The Adventure of the Engineer's Thumb). While men often carried a handkerchief in their pocket ("The Adventure of the Lion's Mane), some, taking the habit from the military, (1) carried it in their sleeve ("The Adventure of the Blanched Soldier"), and others, such as gypsies, tied large ones around their heads ("The Adventure of the Speckled Band").

The humble handkerchief has a long history, although its contemporary use did not appear until the fifteenth century when the Dutch philosopher Erasmus noted that using one's sleeve for such a purpose was boorish. (2) Chinese sculptures from the Chou dynasty (1122 BCE) displayed a decorative cloth head covering, assumed for protection from the sun. Among the early Chinese exports were silk handkerchiefs. The Japanese have used *"hankachi"* since the ninth century. (3) Romans used squares to wipe away sweat (*sudariums*) and threw them to start gladiator games. (4) They became a fashion accessory by the end of the seventeenth century. (5) Originally arriving as a kerchief (a covering for the head), the handkerchief (to be held instead of worn) appeared in the 1500s. (6)

Handkerchiefs became an important means of sending messages, especially where romance was concerned. Knights would indicate their love by tying a handkerchief to the back of their helmets. A young lady would drop her handkerchief for a young man to retrieve. Should the gentleman keep it, he declared his love for her. She might also send him one she embroidered herself or a singed one to declare her burning passion for the man. Should she catch his eye, she might hold it in the middle to indicate a late-night meeting. He would wave his own in response, to show he'd gotten the message. Returning the object later broke off a relationship. (7)

Popularity for the item continued throughout Europe from the 1500s into the twentieth century. Italian designs were the most desirable. They were made with the finest fabrics and were embellished with needle lace. These were often scented with perfume and could be held over the nose and mouth to combat foul odors. (Of course, Holmes scented his with creosote in *The Sign of the Four*.) By the late 1500s, they were so valuable, they were listed in wills, used in dowries, and given as presents to nobility. (8) They also grew in size to the point that King Louis XVI of France declared no one could have one larger than his. (9)

The pocket square became a men's fashion staple in the late 19th century with the introduction of the two-piece suit. Men didn't want their clean handkerchief mixed in with coins, etc. in their pockets and moved the cloth to their upper outside breast pocket. (10) The fashion trend began in England and spread from there, in part, from their use by actors such as Cary Grant and Gary Cooper. While not required for a formal suit, many men still wear one in their jackets. (11) These are distinguished today from a normal handkerchief by a rolled hem and can be worn in several different styles (from a flat square running parallel to the pocket edge to a puff that shows more). (12)

Despite continued use in men's suits, the handkerchief itself is no longer the fixture it once was. Its demise began with the introduction of paper tissue. "Gayetty's Medical Paper" (a brown, rough, thin paper that continued to be available in parts of Europe through the 1970s), appeared in 1857, but the tissue paper recognized today was not developed until 1920. Kimberly-Clark produced a disposable, soft, absorbent paper developed by "creping" (a process of microfolding) that broke down the paper fibers. (13) The company introduced Kleenex, first as a means of removing cold cream, and later for blowing one's nose, with the slogan, "Don't carry a cold in your pocket." (14) Although handkerchiefs have, for the most part, disappeared in the US, they remain popular in Japan. Most Japanese carry at least one or two, primarily for drying one's hands in public restrooms, wiping one's face on a hot day, and covering one's mouth and nose in the event of a fire. (15)

As the Japanese demonstrate, the lowly handkerchief still proves its usefulness in a variety of ways—just as it did more than a hundred years ago.

1. https://www.bloomsburyfashioncentral. com/ products/berg-fashion-library/dictionary/the-dictionary-of-fashion-history/ handkerchief
2. https://hankybook.com/ hankybook-blog/
3. https://topdrawershop.com/ blogs/ blog/ why-carrying-a-handkerchief-never-went- out-of-style-in-japan

4. https://www.shpgroup.eu/tips/from-the-history-of-handkerchiefs/
5. https://www.shpgroup.eu/tips/from-the-history-of-handkerchiefs/
6. https://www.etymonline.com/word/ handkerchief
7. https://hankybook.com/hankybook-blog/
8. http://margaretroedesigns.com/wp-content/uploads/HandkerchiefHist.pdf
9. https://hankybook.com/hankybook-blog/
10. https://www.rampleyandco.com/ pages/the-history-of-the-pocket-square
11. https://www.studiosuits.com/blog/ looking-back-history-pocket-squares/
12. https://www.aristocracy.london/how-to-fold-your-pocket-square/
13. https://www.valmet.com/media/articles/ tissue/the-history-of-tissue-products/
14. https://www.heraldbanner.com/ opinion/columns/on-second-thought-pass-me-a-kleenex-interesting-history-of-tissues-handkerchiefs/article_ff685e36-42a3-11e9-838e-bbf1c1cfaa20.html
15. why-carrying-a-handkerchief-never-went-out-of-style-in-japan

Making An Impression

I n *The Sign of the Four*, Sherlock Holmes mentions his monograph on the use of plaster of paris to preserve footprint impressions. The gypsum compound, however, has many uses, some of which are mentioned in the Canon: for casting molds—such as busts of Napoleon—and plastering walls. Perhaps the most common reference to plaster in the cases did not involve the compound at all.

Plaster of paris is calcium sulfate that, when heated and ground to a fine powder, will set up again when water is added. This represents only one of three types of plaster but is the most common. The others are lime plaster, using calcium hydroxide and sand; and cement plaster, combining plaster, sand, Portland cement, and water. (1) If glue is added to the plaster, it creates a surface called gesso that can be used in tempera or oil painting. (2)

Plaster of paris has long been used in construction—from finishing interiors to flourishes on columns or cornices. (3) Until the 1930s, most homes involved lath-and-plaster walls and ceilings (as mentioned in two cases in the Canon). Strips of one-inch-wide wood were nailed onto studs and then covered with about three coats of plaster. The practice declined after drywall became popular. (4)

These white walls gave the name to the compound in the thirteenth century. According to several accounts, King Henry III coined the name after visiting Paris in 1254 and importing the process to England. (5) By the 18th century, most of the gypsum was mined in Montmartre, outside Paris, (6) but other deposits were found in East Sussex in England in 1873. (7)

Plaster of paris has the specific property of not shrinking or cracking when casting molds—such as statues of Napoleon. Because of this feature, not only has it been used for decorative trim, but also for hand and foot castings. While casting babies' feet has been a common practice since ancient Egypt, (8) it wasn't until 1786 that a plaster cast of a footprint was used to solve a crime. A local constable noticed a boot print near the home of a murdered girl. He used a cast of the print to identify the culprit by comparing it with the boots of those who attended her funeral. (9)

A shoe or footprint is a "plastic" print when it is left in mud, snow, or other substance retaining a three-dimensional track. Such prints can be traced to a particular individual because of several traits unique to each person. At its most basic, the print provides the size and make of a particular shoe, narrowing the number of possible suspects and eliminating others. This preliminary characteristic is important enough for the FBI to maintain a database of sole patterns. To link a shoe print to a particular individual, the wear pattern is used. Each person has his/her own manner of walking (more weight on the heel, more on the ball, etc.) and wears out shoe soles differently. In addition, cuts or nicks on the sole will leave marks in the print. An investigator can compare the plaster cast to a suspect's shoe to determine if they match or not. (10)

Plaster is also mentioned in *A Study in Scarlet, The Valley of Fear,* "The Man with the Twisted Lip," and "The Adventure of the Greek Interpreter" in reference to a very different item. Plasters are also medicinal compounds applied to the skin (for example "mustard plaster"). (11) In 1880, a pharmacist spread a rubber-like substance over gauze to cover the skin and hold a salve in place and termed it "Guttaplaste." (12) Sticking plaster soon entered the market and appears in the Canon as an adhesive tape used to cover cuts, as well as to disfigure Neville St. Clair's and Paul Kratides' face and cover Kratides' mouth to keep him from talking.

Whether distorting a person's features or forming a cast of Napoleon or a suspect's footprint, plaster has quite an "impressive" history.

---

1. https://cementanswers.com/who-invented -plaster-of-paris/
2. https://www.britannica.com/technology / plaster-of-paris
3. https://ourpastimes.com/plaster-of-paris-history-13401651.html
4. https://www.thespruce.com /plaster-and-lath-came-before-drywall-1822861
5. https://history.physio/ plaster-of-paris/
6. https://peternewburysblog.wordpress. com/2012/10/14/why-gypsum-was-mined-at-montmartre/2010/jun/17/south-downs-gypsum-mining
7. https://www.handprints.in/single-post /2017/11/06/history-of-hand-and-foot-impressions
8. http://www.iowaiai.org/about/forensics /footwear/
9. D.P. Lyle *Forensics for Dummies*. Hoboken, NJ: John Wiley and Sons, Inc., 2019.
10. https://www.etymonline.com/word /plaster
11. http://www.fundinguniverse.com /company-histories/beiersdorf-ag-history/

It's a Gas, Gas, Gas

I n several cases, Holmes and Watson enjoyed a whiskey and soda, and once they offered a client a brandy and soda—most likely supplied from the "spirit case" (or tantalus) and gasogene in a corner of the apartment at 221B. Both were common items for the well-supplied gentleman, with soda, or seltzer, water having a long history of providing both refreshment as well as, at times, medicinal properties.

Some mineral springs create carbonated water on their own. Filtered through porous layers of rocks and minerals, the water becomes infused with sodium or potassium for its fizz. Ancient populations often considered these as religious sites, (1) and with healing properties. People would come to "take the waters," soaking in or drinking from the springs to cure almost any disease. (2)

Hippocrates was the first to advocate such springs for medical purposes. (3) He argued that disease involved an imbalance of bodily fluids. To restore balance, treatment involved bathing, drinking water, and exercise and massage. Both private and public baths were constructed, and the Romans spread the concept as they conquered Europe. The British town of Bath was originally a Roman structure.

Following the fall of the Roman Empire, "taking the waters" fell out of popularity, only to be rediscovered during the Renaissance. In the late 1500s, the Italians were once again bathing and drinking spring water to relieve various complaints. One compendium listed more than 78 ailments that could be treated in the baths. (4) The interest in such springs spread across Europe, with a mineral spring in Spa, Belgium giving a name to such facilities. (5)

In the 1700s, water from such springs became commercialized. The most famous of these is Nieder Seltzer, a town outside Frankfurt. Not only did the town supply the name "seltzer" to the water, it also was the first to export it to the US in three-pint stone bottles. These were corked and sealed to maintain the effervescence. Once uncorked, however, all the gas escaped within a day, leaving behind a flat, noticeably saltier water behind. (6)

Given the limited supply of natural mineral waters, others sought means of carbonating regular water. John Priestly is given credit for inventing carbonated water in 1767 by suspending a bowl of water over a beer vat (which produces carbon dioxide) in Leeds, England. A feasible production process was introduced in 1781 when Thomas Henry in Manchester, England created the first carbonated water factory. (7)

In addition to commercially produced soda-water, homemade options were also developed—such as the gasogene in Holmes' possession. This particular device consisted of two glass globes covered in wire mesh for protection from broken glass and connected to each other through a tube. Tartaric acid (from grapes) and bicarbonate of soda were mixed in the lower orb and still water was placed in the upper. Once the gasogene was assembled, water dripped into the lower part to create a chemical reaction between the alkali and the acid, forming a gas, which was forced up the tube and into the water to create carbonated water. (8)

One of the byproducts of such carbonation is carbonic acid, which gives the water a tart taste and also kills bacteria. This provides an additional reason as a healthful substitute before chlorinating became common practice. While many drank seltzer water alone because of the touted medicinal properties (basically, clean water), others also used it for mixing with drinks, such as whiskey or brandy, as mentioned by Holmes. Other drinks were also produced with seltzer or soda water. Beeton's *Book of Household Management* included four drink recipes requiring soda-water (Champagne Cup, anyone?), as well as noting its benefits for the sick. (9)

When Holmes and Watson enjoy their whiskey and soda, they are participating in a ritual that dates far back into history.

If you'd like to see a gasogene in action, here's a video:
http://www.thisvictorianlife.com/blog/archives/11-2019

1. https://sparklingcbd.com/beverage-blog/the-surprising-history-of-carbonated-water
2. https://www.theatlantic.com/science/archive/2016/12/gettin-fizzy-with-it/510470/#main-content
3. https://facesspa.com/blog/where-the-word-spa-comes-from/
4. https://ard.bmj.com/content/61/3/273
5. https://facesspa.com/blog/where-the-word-spa-comes-from/
6. Oliver Oldschool, *The Portfolio*. Philadelphia: Bradford and Inskeep, 1809, page 312.
7. https://www.seltzernation.com/the-history-of-seltzer-water/
8. https://www.youtube.com/watch?v=_5PW4FvLPfw&t=10s
9. Isabella Beeton, *Book of Household Management*. London: Ward, Lock and Company, 1898

That Voodoo You Do So Well

I n "The Adventure of Wisteria Lodge," Sherlock, Watson, and Inspector Baynes found some rather odd items in a house's kitchen: a human figure with a shell belt, a dead white cock, a pail of blood, and charred bones. Based on these findings, Baynes arrested Garcia's cook for his employer's murder to lure the actual perpetrator from hiding. Holmes explained the cook's objects were related to an animal sacrifice made to appease the gods before attempting an important activity. While Holmes indicated he had researched the practice at the British Museum, the description had little to do with true voodoo rituals and more about misinformation commonly reported in the 1800s.

The origins of vodou—the currently preferred spelling—are traced back to Haiti, (1) although it incorporates much of vodun, a West African religion practiced by about 30 million people. (2) In addition to a supreme being, Bondye, other spirits (lwa or loa) have dominion over various parts of life, and depending on the worshiper's needs, offerings are made to the spirit controlling that aspect—such as a farmer would focus on the spirit of agriculture, or one desiring love to another spirit. When those from West Africa were brought to

Haiti, Brazil, Cuba, and Louisiana as slaves, they incorporated aspects of this religion into Roman Catholicism when their owners "converted" them. Over time, many of the spirits became associated with Christian saints. (3)

Offerings to these spirits can include animal sacrifice, a practice appearing in many religions including Islam and Hinduism. When such sacrifices are made in vodou, the animal is then cooked and shared among members, primarily the poor. (4) Current practices are moving away from such sacrifices although they may still occur in more rural areas. A high priestess in New Orleans, a vegan, has reported no problem completing her rituals without such traditions. (5)

Similarly, the use of fetishes has been misrepresented. Talismans used for medicine or spiritual power can be found in West African markets and may include statues or dolls representing gods and dried animal parts. (6) The elaborately crafted images provide a personal connection to the spirits and have no purpose related to harming or controlling another person. (7)

Perhaps the most misunderstood aspect of vodou religion is spiritual possession. While some religions view such practices as evil, vodou practitioners seek such an experience. The belief is that a soul can leave a body during possession, with a spirit replacing it and creating a sort of religious frenzy. Such control is different from zombies who lack their soul and can be controlled by bokors by magical means and have no resemblance to the human-eating monsters in current films. (8)

The origin of such distorted views of vodou practices can be traced back to Victorian publications providing second-hand accounts of such activities. While the actual events have been obscured by time, a trial in Haiti in 1864 condemned eight men and women to death for the murder and cannibalism of a young girl. European papers carried the story, and Sir Spenser St. John repeated the trial's particulars in his memoir of his period as the British Consul-General in Haiti. (9) Another Briton, James Froude, reported incidents of serpent worship and animal and child sacrifice a priest shared with him in 1888. (10) William Newell, however, suggested these accounts were "myths," comparing the description—and even the name—to practices of a European sect in the fifteenth century. (11)

While Holmes recognized the items the cook left in the kitchen as part of a vodou ritual, he depended on Eckermann's treatise to provide the meaning and practice behind them, repeating the misconceptions prevalent in Victorian England and perpetuated today in Hollywood. The facts regarding the cook's activities cleared him of any involvement in the murder, just as understanding vodou's true beliefs and customs would strip the practice of its maligned mystique.

---

1. https://www.livescience.com/40803-voodoo-facts.html
2. https://www.npr.org/templates/story/ story.php? storyId=1666721
3. https://www.livescience.com/40803-voodoo-facts.html
4. https://slate.com/culture/2013/11 /anthony-karen-a-photographers-look-inside-a-haitian-voodoo-ritual-photos.html
5. https://www.vice.com/en/article gvmnwb/the-vegan-vodou-high-priestess-of-new-orleans-isnt-interested-in-animal-sacrifice
6. https://www.npr.org/templates/story/ story.php? storyId=1666721
7. https://macaulay.cuny.edu/seminars /lutton07/articles/v/o/d/Vodou.html
8. https://www.livescience.com/40803-voodoo-facts.html
9. https://www.smithsonianmag.com/ history/the-trial-that-gave-vodou-a-bad-name-83801276/

10. James Anthony Froude, *The English in the West Indies*, London: Longmans, Green, and Co. 1888, page 303.
11. William Newell, "Myths of Voodoo Worship and Child Sacrifice in Hayti," *The Journal of American Folklore*, Vol. 1, No. 1, 1888, pages 16-30.

Take Your Breath Away

In "The Adventure of the Sussex Vampire," Sherlock Holmes determined a mother, the accused vampire, was actually sucking a toxin from her child's neck. The boy had been wounded with a poisoned (most likely curare) arrow. His half-brother had stolen the weapon from their father's collection of South American artifacts. Curare had a long history in the Americas, and knowledge of the poison traveled back to Europe almost from its discovery. Its secrets, however, took centuries to uncover, and its medical uses appeared only within the last one hundred years.

Curare, or *Chondrdendron tomentosum*, is a woody vine that grows in the South American jungles. In addition to the primary metabolites produced to make the plant grow, it also creates secondary metabolites, the alkaloid D-tubocurarine, that serves as a defense mechanism. D-tubocuraine is a neurotoxin that causes paralysis when it enters the bloodstream. (1) Paralysis occurs from interference with the contraction of the muscle cells, beginning with extremities such as the toes, ears, and eyes with a progression to the neck and limbs, and finally, those controlling respiration. Without intervention, death will occur. (2) The rate of fatality depends upon the size of the animal. Birds perish within one to two minutes, small mammals up to ten minutes, and large mammals up to 20 minutes. (3) All the while, the victim is conscious and feeling all that is occurring, but unable to move. (4)

European explorers learned of indigenous use of curare soon after discovering the New World. Warriors attacked Christopher Columbus' crew during a land excursion, and two died very quickly after what appeared to be minor arrow wounds. A brown paste was found on the tips, indicating the weapons carried poison. Conflicts between the English, Spanish, and Portuguese, however, limited additional examinations of the substance until the 1700s when samples were brought to Europe and used in various experiments, including one that found using a bellows to inflate the lungs kept the victim alive until the toxin dissipated. (5)

At the end of the 18th century, Alexander von Humboldt spent five years in South America and studied curare preparation with an indigenous healer. Among the wisdom learned was that curare had no effect when ingested, only becoming effective when it penetrated the skin. (6) As a result curare could be handled without incident if the skin was unbroken. The meat of poisoned animals could even be eaten without harm. Additionally, paralysis could be avoided if the poison was sucked from the wound. The one removing the toxin, however, needed to be free of sores or cuts in the mouth to avoid their own paralysis. (7)

Experimentation into the uses of curare continued into the 19th and 20th centuries. Of particular note was Richard Gill who brought back 25 pounds of curare and botanical samples in the hopes of finding a cure for his own infirmity (possibly multiple sclerosis). He provided them to E.R. Squib and Sons for research. While never finding the answer to Gill's medical issues, researchers did identify its usefulness as a muscle relaxant during surgery. In WWII, a combination of a curare derivative and anesthesia was found to facilitate operations. (8)

As a native of South America, Mrs. Ferguson—the Sussex

Vampire—would have been familiar with curare and how those indigenous to the area sucked the toxin from a victim to save their life. As Holmes noted, this wife imitated yet another woman of Spanish descent. Queen Eleanor sucked venom from the arm of Edward I when he was wounded with a poisoned knife. In the case of Mrs. Ferguson, Holmes' recognized both her knowledge and courage. She preferred to put herself in jeopardy not only by drawing out the poison from her son but also by accepting the title of "vampire" rather than upset her husband by exposing the true culprit—the older brother.

------

1. https://sites.evergreen.edu/ plantchemeco/ curare-a-cure-all-kill-all-plant/

2. https://www.britannica.com/science/ curare

3. http://web.pdx.edu/~fischerw/proj_pub / humboldt_project/docs/0101-0125/0123c_Gibson_curare.pdf

4. Lawrence Altman, *Who Goes First?* Berkeley: University of California Press. 1986, page 75.

5. Thandia Ragnavendra, "Neuromuscular blocking drugs: discovery and development," *Journal of the Royal Society of Medicine*, 95: July 2002, page 363.

6. https://www.ncbi.nlm.nih.gov/pmc/articles/PM-C4237325/#pone.0112026-Gomsu1

7. Lawrence Altman, *Who Goes First?* Berkeley: University of California Press. 1986, page 75.

8. Ragnavendra, page 364.

Victorian Addictions

Holmes' cocaine use was well-known. Shortly after moving in together, Watson suspected Holmes of using some narcotic. In *The Sign of the Four,* he warned him cocaine use involved increased tissue change, and he reported he did successfully "wean him from that...mania" in "The Adventure of the Missing Three-Quarter." Watson's efforts to treat his companion's drug use reflected a change in perspective concerning the public's growing dependence on such substances. No longer a matter of willpower, the medical community accepted it as a disease by the end of the 1800s, even applying a new term: "addiction."

While cocaine was Holmes' drug of choice, Victorians, in general, consumed a great number of addictive substances. These included alcohol, opium, cannabis, coca, mescal, and, around the middle of the 1800s and the introduction of the hypodermic needle, morphine and heroin. (1) All were available over the counter from a pharmacist or in commercial products designed for everyone from babies to adults. Few considered it more than a "habit"—at least for themselves—as illustrated in this note by a long-time morphine user:

> I have myself been in the habit of taking morphia for thirty years. I
> began by taking chlorodyne for a spasmodic complaint, as ordered
> by two eminent medical men. It was changed by my husband for

morphia, with the result that by constantly increasing the dose it came at last to 4 scruples per week, which has been the regular quantity taken now for very many years.

This medicine-so deleterious in most instances-has by no means impaired the vitality of my system, or tended in any degree to reduce my activity, which is equal to that of many young women, although I am now 67 years of age.

My enjoyment of life is perfect, and I have none of the haggard, emaciated look borne by most persons who adopt this treatment. My eyes are black and bright, the sight being no worse than that of most persons my age.

The only evil which appears to arise from the use of this medicine is a considerable increase of fat, and I should be considerably obliged if any of your contributors will kindly inform me if this increase of adipose tissue is a natural result of the morphia.

I am, sir, yours faithfully, E.L.P.B. (2)

While the 1888 letter-writer noted no ill effects for herself, she did recognize that not all were so fortunate. Most did, as she described, experience "deleterious" effects. By this point, the medical community recognized addiction as a problem, and a shift occurred toward defining it as a disease.

Continued drug use first creates a tolerance (requiring a higher dose for the same effect) and then a physical dependence (exhibited by withdrawal symptoms). These consequences were noted as early as the 1500s in Europe. Only a certain percentage of those experiencing these symptoms, however, actually continue to a true addiction—a chronic disorder that hijacks brain circuits and leads to a preference for immediate rewards despite negative consequences. (3)

While the behavior and symptoms of chronic alcohol use had been observed since ancient times, the term "addiction" as applied to such dependence only entered the medical vocabulary around the 1900s, replacing terms such as inebriety. Prior to the 19th century, the term *addictus* referred to a person who was enslaved (turned over to a master) to work off unpaid debts. (4) The shift to this phrase for dependent substance use indicated a change in perspective—the user had been "enslaved" by the substance. Watson even used the term to portray Isa Whitney's opium use in "The Man with the Twisted Lip."

While Dr. Nicolaes Tulp and Cornelius Bontekoe used a disease model to explain the loss of control over alcohol intake in the 1600s, (5) the paradigm did not enter the medical literature until the end of the 19th century. Dr. Benjamin Rush in the US and Dr. Thomas Trotter in the UK documented the physical effects of long-term alcohol use (the most prevalent substance at the time) on different organs, such as the liver, as well as chronic users' mortality rates. Thomas Davison Crothers expanded on these concepts in the late 1800s in a series of books that addressed the physical effects of different substances. The 20th century saw a rise in the medical community in further identifying and defining addictions as a disease, including such prominent organizations as the World Health Organization and the American Medical Association. Later, sophisticated equipment not previously available was able to document changes in the brain, marking it as a disease. (6)

Watson specifically refers to Holmes' addictions twice: to "some" narcotic in *A Study in Scarlet* and to making or listening to music at strange hours in *The Adventure of the Dying Detective*. He was able to cure his friend of the first but never reported any success with the second.

----

1. https://wellcomecollection.org/articles/
   W87wthIAACQizfap
2. Wife of a British pharmacist quoted in https://
   www.cambridge.org/core/services/aop-cambridge-
   core/content/view/ 68A05F992DC15DE8BA9-
   CADACF6F6449 A/S0025727300040321a.pdf/div-

class-title-development-of-the-disease-model-of-drug-
addiction-in-britain-1870-1926-div.pdf

3. https://www.psychologytoday.com/us/blog/the-gravity-
weight/202009/the-opium-eaters

4. https://www.ncbi.nlm.nih.gov/pmc/articles/PMC3202501/

5. *Ibid*

6. https://commons.nmu.edu/cgi/viewcontent.cgi?
article=1109&context=theses

A Compass Points the Way

In "The Adventure of the Red-Headed League," Holmes noted Jabez Wilson was a Freemason because he wore an arc-and-compass breastpin. Similarly, in "The Adventure of the Norwood Builder," both Holmes and Watson identified John McFarlane as a Freemason because of a watch charm. While Freemasonry can trace its roots back to at least the 14th century, the fraternal organization as it is known today developed in the early 1700s in England and Scotland (1) when the first Grand Lodge was formed in 1717. (2)

The compass on Wilson's breastpin (and most likely part of McFarlane's watch-charm)—along with the square—appears in Freemasonry's most common symbols and represents the organization's origins. Ancient architectural tools such as the compass and square were used to make straight lines and angles. (3) In the center the letter G will often be included, although various meanings have been attributed to the letter, including "geometry," and "God." (4) Current Masonic teachings note that the compass represents one's relationships with others, as being honorable and truthful. The square represents self-control. Together, one leads a "true and virtuous" life. (5)

Freemason origins are shrouded in mystery. While stone masons were employed in the building of Egypt's pyramids and the temple in Jerusalem, stone masons did not organize into guilds until the Middle

Ages as a means of controlling their craft. As demand for cathedrals declined, the guilds began to accept non-working members to maintain their ranks. As the honorary members dominated the organization, the lodges shifted into the speculative Freemasonry recognized today. (6) Just as with the guilds, where new workers entered as apprentices to learn their trade, Masons today pass through three "degrees" of membership: Apprentice, Fellow Craft (skilled member), and Master Mason. (7)

Four lodges in England joined to create the Premier Grand Lodge of England in 1717, becoming the focal point of British Masonry with its members spreading across Europe and beyond as new lodges formed in both the North American colonies (George Washington was a Mason) as well as far east as Russia. (8) The Premier Grand Lodge introduced the first degree (Master Mason) above the Fellow Craft, and additional high degrees followed, identified as Scottish degrees (referring to the rites, not Scotland itself). French Masonry, however, added even more degrees, described by Etienne Morin in 1763 in his manuscript *Order of the Royal Secret*. When Morin traveled to Jamaica, he empowered another Mason, Henry Andrew Francken to establish lodges in the colonies. Francken also translated Morin's manuscript into English, which created the basis for the Scottish Rite appendant organization operating primarily in North America in 1768. (9)

Part of the mystery of Freemasonry involves both these rites as well as the symbolism running through the organization. Development and use of such symbols related to the masonry craft before widespread literacy. While common to various lodges and countries, the meaning may shift between them. True Freemason scholars spend time studying these symbols for their deeper meaning within their society. Some of the most common include acacia wood, the double-headed eagle, the blazing star, the lamb, the gavel, the sheaf of corn, and the eye. Additionally, specific dress is worn at meetings and other gatherings. These include the apron, the cable tow, and blue shoes or slippers. (10) Freemasons also greet and know each other with special handshakes based on their rank within the organization. (11)

While certain aspects of the society—such as particular rituals—are shared only with members (and at times only with those of a certain rank), Masons do not keep their membership secret, and many are well-known, including US presidents and a certain literary agent by the name of Arthur Conan Doyle. Neither did Jabez Wilson or John McFarlane, making it relatively easy for Holmes to recognize their affiliation.

---

1. https://www.livescience.com/ freemasons.html
2. https://beafreemason.org/faq
3. https://www.masonic-lodge-of-education.com/square-and- compasses.html
4. https://www.history.com/news/freemasons-facts-symbols-handshake-meaning
5. https://beafreemason.org/masonic-life
6. https://www.britannica.com/biography/Clement-XII
7. https://beafreemason.org/degrees
8. https://www.livescience.com/freemasons.html
9. https://scottishrite.org/about/history/
10. https://www.masonic-lodge-of-education.com/freemason-symbols.html
11. https://www.history.com/news/freemasons-facts-symbols-handshake-meaning

While Holmes' tweed deerstalker shown in Paget's illustrations was never mentioned in the actual writings, he did wear a tweed coat in *The Hound of the Baskervilles* and a tweed suit in "A Scandal in Bohemia." Other men were described as wearing tweed suits in eight other cases, but the mere mention of this very popular weave was enough to evoke in the reader's mind the image of the man's suit.

Scottish farmers developed the cloth, called Clò-Mór (meaning "the big cloth") in the 1700s to protect them from the elements. Woven by hand, the fabric is a natural fiber (virgin wool) in a soft, open weave, that originally was quite thick and not as colorful or intricately designed as now. (1) The wool, from Cheviot sheep, produced garments that were warm, waterproof, and thick. The threads were dyed with natural plant colors such as lichens. (2)

By the 1830s, the British aristocracy was using the fabric for their staff uniforms with specially commissioned patterns for their country estates. (3) Unique designs were used to distinguish those from the different estates during hunting and other outdoor activities. Not only were the garments weather-resistant, the patterns' natural dyes served as camouflage. (4) The most famous of these estate tweeds was the granite and crimson heather "Balmoral Tweed" created by Prince Albert after purchasing Balmoral castle in 1853. (5)

While some attribute the fabric's name to the Tweed River, most references agree that its moniker developed by accident. The Scottish word for twill is *tweel*, and in 1826, a London milliner misread the label on a shipment of wool tweel and advertised the arrival of tweed fabric. The name stuck and has been used ever since. (6)

In the mid-1800s, automation increased production, and demand for the fabric reached beyond the aristocracy. While men's fashions included tweed jackets, suits, and other accessories such as hats, by the early 1860s, women also included tweed in their wardrobe. As they pursued outdoor sports such as walking, shooting, and cycling, they often wore jackets, cloaks, coats, and, later, matching jackets and skirts for informal or sporting wear. (7)

To protect themselves from the rise in automated tweed mills, the self-employed weavers in the Outer Hebrides formed the Harris Tweed Authority in 1909 to safeguard the cloth and patterns from imitation. Shielded by an Act of Parliament, only that fabric sanctioned by the Authority can carry the certification of hand-woven Harris tweed. (8)

In addition to Harris tweed, other popular tweeds can be characterized by their weave, the type of sheep, or their origin. Included among these are:

- Donegal tweed from the Irish Donegal County with rainbow specks of yarn in its knobby surface
- Saxony tweed originating from Saxony, Germany, and made with merino wool
- Herringbone tweed uses a weave that forms a V pattern on the surface similar to fish bones
- Shetland tweed hails from the Shetland Islands and is characterized by a lighter, more delicate wool
- Barleycorn tweed sports bumpy "barleycorn kernels" along its surface
- Cheviot tweed is a rougher and heavier fabric from the Cheviot Hills

- Overcheck twill uses a plain twill pattern with an overlaid check design (9)

In the early 1900s, tweed reached worldwide popularity. Coco Chanel raised it to haute couture in the 1920s by incorporating it into her designs, and it reached the world's pinnacle when Sir Edmund Hillary wore it when he ascended Mount Everest. (10)

With a shift in fashions, tweed's popularity plummeted, and Harris tweed production in 2006 had dropped 90% from its peak in the 1960s. Mills closed, and workers lost their jobs following an effort by one businessman to corner the market on Harris tweed. When his venture failed, efforts by two other businessmen to revive the industry emerged. Of great concern was the loss of the centuries of patterns that the first businessman had eliminated. More than eight thousand of these designs were found in a warehouse, preserving this rich tradition, and Harris tweed is again winning export awards. (11)

It was not happenstance that Holmes wore a tweed coat while roaming the Dartmoor moors. Not only did it protect him from the elements, it also helped him blend into the surroundings—perfect for observing without being observed. One must wonder, however, if it was a houndstooth weave.

---

1. https://www.josephturner.co.uk/ customer/ pages/about/what_is_tweed
2. https://www.nationalgeographic.com/ travel/article/tweed-weaves-tales-of-scottish-history-and-landscapes
3. https://www.josephturner.co.uk/ customer/pages/about/what_is_tweed
4. https://www.britannica.com/topic/ tweed
5. https://www.masterclass.com/articles /what-is-tweed#8-different-types-of-tweed

6. https://www.nationalgeographic.com/ travel/article/tweed-weaves-tales-of-scottish-history-and-landscapes

7. https://fashion-history.lovetoknow. com/fabrics-fibers/tweed

8. https://clan.com/blog/history-of-tweed

9. https://www.masterclass.com/articles/ what-is-tweed#8-different-types-of-tweed

10. https://www.nationalgeographic.com/ travel/article/tweed-weaves-tales-of-scottish-history-and-landscapes

11. https://clan.com/blog/history-of-tweed

Mark of a Sinner or a Saint? British Attitudes Toward Leprosy

In "The Adventure of the Blanched Soldier," the fear that Godfrey Emsworth had contracted leprosy while in South Africa was enough for the family to isolate the poor man completely from all society. While their fears were misplaced, the actual disease—ichthyosis or pseudo-leprosy—offered a rather grim prognosis as well. Public opinion of the second, however, lacked the stigma carried with the first.

Humans have been aware of leprosy, or Hansen's disease, since ancient times, with references to the illness appearing even in the Bible. Caused by a bacterial infection, the ailment is marked by pale-colored skin sores and lumps or bumps that do not disappear. As the disease progresses, it attacks the nerves, leading to a loss of feeling in the arms and legs and muscle weakness. Despite being contagious, it is difficult to contract the disease. Infection only occurs after repeated exposure to nasal or mouth droplets and the incubation period (when

70

symptoms appear) can be from three to five years to up to twenty years. (1)

While leprosy's source is not known, traditional theories suggest it might have originated in India, Africa, or the Middle East. More recent research of ancient European burial sites indicates its existence on the continent much earlier than previously believed. The same strains have been found in current squirrel populations, leading to the belief that the spread may have been related to Viking squirrel fur traders. (2)

Despite the presence of the same disease as in ancient times, European infections peaked in the mid-1500s. Leprosy was so common throughout medieval Europe, it was estimated that one in 30 were infected. With no change in the illness' genetic makeup, researchers theorize that present Europeans have developed a genetic resistance to the disease. (3)

Beliefs about leprosy date back to Biblical times. The Hebrew term for several different skin diseases, *tzaraat*, rendered an individual ritually unclean and required physical separation from the community to avoid its moral contamination. *Tzaraat* was later translated into Greek as *lepra* and serves as the basis for the current term *leprosy*. (4) The term, however, did not refer to what is now recognized as leprosy, which was referred to as *elephantiasis Graecorum*. (5)

Although the skin diseases referred to as leprosy in the European Middle Ages had no relation to the Biblical ailments, the public reaction to it mirrored ancient beliefs, split between it being a punishment for sin or enduring a living purgatory. With the lepers' suffering mimicking that of Christ, they would immediately enter Heaven. In addition, those who tended to the diseased would also reduce their own time in purgatory. As a result, at least 320 leper, or lazar, houses were established in England alone, with more across all of Europe. When infections suddenly dropped in the 16th century and concern over other contagious diseases (such as the Black Death) increased, those infected faced greater restrictions and isolation. (6)

The late nineteenth century saw a re-emergence of leprosy as a humanitarian cause, not only in England but across the British Empire. Numerous societies were formed to provide support for those suffering from the disease—particularly in India and Africa. Hospitals and colonies where the infected could live out their days, and converted to Christianity, were funded through several missionary societies into the 1930s. Fundraising efforts focused on the stigma associated with those affected. (7)

Given the image of the leper presented in contemporary publicity at the end of the 1800s, the family's reaction to Godfrey Emsworth's own affliction would have been a common one. The alternative diagnosis of his condition by Holmes' doctor, then, provided a great relief to the family. Ichthyosis, or pseudo-leprosy, presents with similar symptoms as true leprosy.

Ichthyosis is most often caused by a genetic mutation and appears as early as infancy. The skin disease appears as dry, scaly skin that can be extra-thick or thin. The term comes from the Greek word, "ichthy," meaning fish, and refers to the skin forming scales resembling those of fish. (8) That Emsworth contracted the disease later in life suggests his condition was acquired ichthyosis, which has very different underlying causes. It is associated with malignancies, different diseases (including leprosy), and certain medication use. In addition, while the skin can be treated to relieve the symptoms, no cure exists for the sufferer. (9)

While Emsworth's second diagnosis might have saved him and his family from the stigma of leprosy, his true diagnosis was not an end to his problems. The actual disease presented a new set of medical problems with very serious consequences.

---

1. https://www.webmd.com/skin-problems -and-treatments/guide/leprosy-symptoms -treatments-history

2. https://www.smithsonianmag.com/ smart-news/did-leprosy-originate-europe-180969061/

3. https://www.npr.org/sections/health-shots/2013/06/13/191337793/scientists-go- medieval-to-solve-ancient-leprosy-puzzle

4. A Grzybowki, M. Nita, "Leprosy in the Bible," *Clinics in Dermatology*, Vol 34, Issue 1, 2016, pp 3-7.

5. https://www.encyclopedia.com/religion /encyclopedias-almanacs-transcripts-and-maps /leprosy-bible

6. https://historicengland.org.uk/research /inclusive-heritage/ disability-history/1050-1485/time-of-leprosy/

7. K. Vongsathorn. "Gnawing Pains, Festering Ulcers, and Nightmare Suffering: Selling Leprosy as a Humanitarian Cause in the British Empire, c. 1890-1960." *The Journal of imperial and commonwealth history* vol. 40,5 (2012): 863-878.

8. https://www.firstskinfoundation.org /what-is-ichthyosis

9. https://www.jaad.org/article /S0190-9622(06)01222-9/fulltext#:~:text=Ac-quired%20ichthyosis%20(AI)%20is%20a,infec-tious%20diseases%3B%20and%20medication%20use.

A Not-So-Gentlemanly Game of Cards

T he card game whist lay behind two deaths in the Canon: Ronald Adair's in "The Adventure of the Empty House" and Brenda Tregennis' in "The Adventure of the Devil's Foot." Colonel Sabastian Moran shot Adair when he confronted him about cheating at the card game, and Brenda Tregennis died while playing the game after inhaling fumes from a poisonous root. Despite such deadly consequences, whist was the most popular card game among Victorian elite.

Card playing has a long history, with the first recorded in China around 800 CE, and gambling even longer (more than 4000 years ago). (1) Whist's lifespan, on the other hand, was rather short, spanning a period between the 1700s to the 1900s when it was superseded by bridge. (2)

Originally a game for common men, whist gained in popularity when gentlemen took it up for amusement at coffee houses and carried it into their clubs. The game became associated with strategy and mental skills and, thus, appropriate for the upper classes. (3) To play, and win, required "a good memory, sympathetic partnering, and psychological acumen." Players also developed strategies to cheat despite Edward Hoyle's (the first to set down the rules for the game) condemnation of such actions. (4)

Similar to bridge or spades, whist involved two teams attempting to collect "tricks." The game involved a standard 52-card deck (with the ace being the highest card). Teams were determined by cutting the cards, with the two selecting the highest cards and the other two becoming partners. The cards were shuffled and distributed to each player, with the last card left face up on the table during the first trick (and then returned to the dealer's hand). This card determined the "trump suit" for the game. A card from the trump suit won the trick, regardless of any other card played. The player to the dealer's left began play by setting down a card. The others played a card in the same suit unless they didn't have one. The trick was taken by the highest card, and play continued until all thirteen tricks had been collected. (5)

The team with the most tricks after the round won and was awarded a point for all tricks taken after the first six (called "making book"). Additional points could be won by collecting either three (for two points) or four (four points) of the "honours" (ace, king, queen, and jack in the trump suit). The first team to accumulate ten points (in standard whist) or five (in short whist) won the game. In a "rubber of whist," the winning team was determined by the best of three games. (6)

For the aristocracy, betting on whist games was considered appropriate because it required strategy instead of those depending on chance (provided by dice) preferred by the lower classes. The elite's participation in such games meant the stakes in whist could be high. Bets as great as £100,000—such as those by the Duke of Wellington —were the stuff of legend, (7) and contemporary literature included many morality tales of young aristocrats meeting their ruin from such excesses. (8) This sort of extravagant gambling was viewed as threatening the country's whole social fabric. The aristocracy's wealth and hierarchy were based on land ownership and the size of one's holdings. Gambling losses paid by land transfers could lead to shifts in both property lines and status within the nobility and, thus, endangered the social structure of those in power. (9)

Given such stakes, cheating became a fixture within the clubs. Despite Hoyle's treatise and rules to the contrary, a variety of techniques were available for players to "gain the upper hand." Secret signals, such as a kick under the table, might be passed to one's partner, or through codes disguised as comments during play, such as exclaiming "My dear sir," or including a certain word like "truly" to indicate a particular suit. Signals using an object, for example, a handkerchief, or using a certain number of fingers when playing a card, could inform a partner of a good hand or the number of trump cards possessed. Finally, if skilled in the art of shuffling and dealing, the cheater could control which cards were dealt to him and his partner. (10)

According to Watson, Ronald Adair's own card playing was both honorable and modest. His losses or winnings were well within his income, despite being a member of several clubs and playing almost every day—until he was paired with Colonel Moran and won much more than his usual five pounds. While the technique Moran used to win at the Bagatelle Card Club was not specified, Ronald Adair was clever enough to spot it and paid with his life.

---

1. https://www.gambling.net/history/
2. https://www.britannica.com/topic/whist
3. https://londonhistorians.wordpress.com /2014/06/05/ gambling-in-londons- most-ruinous-gentlemens-clubs/
4. https://regency-explorer.net/whist/
5. https://www.britannica.com/topic/whist
6. https://www.kristenkoster.com/a-regency-primer-on-how-to-play-whist/

7. https://londonhistorians.wordpress.com /2014/06/05/gambling-in-londons-most-ruinous-gentlemens-clubs/
8. https://scholarworks.iu.edu/dspace/handle/2022/25690
9. https://muse.jhu.edu/article/678621/pdf
10. https://regency-explorer.net/whist/

Living on London's Mean Streets

H olmes introduced Watson to the Baker Street Irregulars in their first adventure, *A Study in Scarlet*. At that point, however, Watson referred to them in a common term of the period—"street arabs." Not until *The Sign of the Four* did Holmes provide Watson with their official title: The Baker Street Irregulars. These young boys—six in the first case and a dozen in the second—represented only a small portion of the 35,000 estimated to be living on the London streets in 1902. (1)

The nineteenth century saw London's population explode—from 1 million in 1800 to 6.5 million at its end. This teeming metropolis strained the city's resources, especially in the area of housing. Charles Dickens and Henry Mayhew chronicled the lives of those without housing and barely surviving to raise awareness of the problem, particularly among the young. (2) Around this time, the term "street arab" appeared to describe such homeless children and their nomadic existence. (3)

Those as young as three or four supported their existence either through selling wares, such as shoe blacking, newspapers, or flowers; mudlarking (searching the Thames for refuse during low tide); costermongering (hawking fruits or vegetables for a stall owner); or, perhaps most often, resorting to some criminal activity. (4) Among the lawbreakers, a hierarchy existed. Those at the bottom stole foodstuffs. Sneak thieves were higher on the chain, but below the shoplifter. At the top were the pickpockets and housebreakers. Most were arrested and sent to prison but would be released a while later, only to be arrested again. Prisons did not separate the populations by age, and as a result, younger inmates learned new tricks from older ones. As children continued in their criminal education and career, judges often sentenced those who had been arrested numerous times with increasingly serious offenses to transportation to Australia. (5)

Eighteen fifty-four provided an alternative to imprisonment for juveniles: the Reformatory School. Magistrates could grant a pardon to criminal offenders under the age of 16 if they agreed to spend two to five years at a certified reformatory school after spending 15 days in prison. These schools, primarily run by private charities or religious groups, provided education, trade skills, and, depending on the institution, sports or other recreational activities. (6) Approximately 1000 juveniles were sentenced to reformatories each year during the second half of the 1800s.

An additional 9000 per year were admitted to Industrial schools. (7) Created by reformers through the Industrial Schools Act of 1857, these children were admitted to such institutions without the two-week imprisonment requirement. The schools focused on younger children not sentenced for criminal offenses but at risk for such activity in the future. By 1875, England and Wales had 54 reformatory schools and 82 industrial schools. (8)

The schools were also required to follow those leaving the programs for up to three years. While some appeared to have achieved a proper trade following release, other attendees reported harsh treatment. Corporal punishment was prohibited in new schools created after 1876, but existing schools could continue the use of caning and other disciplinary actions. (9)

The last mention of the Baker Street Irregulars in the Canon identified a new leader for the group. Six years after *The Sign of the*

Four, in "The Crooked Man," Simpson was the head Irregular, with no mention of Wiggins' fate. (10) Given the various options a magistrate or judge had before him, one can speculate Wiggins might have spent time in a reform or industrial school. He most probably was arrested and released several times, and given his leadership skills, might even have been selected for transportation to Australia or another British colony. Some of the boys sent to Australia, Canada, or South Africa created good lives for themselves in these new countries, and Wiggins might have been among those who forged a productive life after leaving the Irregulars, perhaps with even a little help from his mentor, Sherlock Holmes.

---

1. https://leftfootforward.org/2016/03/homelessness-has-returned-to-1900s-levels/
2. https://www.pressreader.com/uk/who-do-you-think-you-are-magazine/20170926/281655370250960
3. https://www.wordsense.eu/street_Arab/
4. https://www.pressreader.com/uk/who-do-you-think-you-are-magazine/20170926/281655370250960
5. J.J. Tobias, *Crime and Police in England 1700-1900.* New York: St. Martin Press, 1979.
6. http://www.childrenshomes.org.uk/Rfy/
7. https://theconversation.com/victorian-child-reformatories-were-more-successful-than-todays-youth-justice-system-85634
8. http://www.childrenshomes.org.uk/Rfy/
9. https://ora.ox.ac.uk/catalog/ uuid:a551dd78-6ebc-4b0d-a2fe-693e74d5e19c/download_file?file_format=application%2Fpdf&safe_ filename=602354922.pdf
10. Steve Doyle and David Crowder, *Sherlock Holmes for Dummies.* Hoboken, NJ: Wiley Publishing, Inc., 2010.

In their first adventure together, Watson identified Holmes as a "first-rate chemist" and described his constant experimentation once they rented their rooms at 221B. From their first meeting, Holmes showed his skills in chemistry when he announced he had just developed a test to determine the presence of blood. In addition, throughout the Canon, he relies on chemical analyses not only as a means of solving a case but also as a form of relaxation. His chemical studies were so well known, the Royal Society of Chemistry awarded him a fellowship in 2002. (1) Not all, however, have as high an opinion of Holmes' abilities as Watson or this Royal Society.

Chemistry refers to changes in the nature of substances, (2) and was first studied more than 4000 years ago by the ancient Egyptians. Muslim scholars continued studies of how matter changed, calling it *al-kimia,* where it returned to Europe as alchemy, the search for transforming baser metals into gold. Chemistry became a proper science in the 1700s with experiments involving the discovery of oxygen among other elements. Later discoveries such as the radioactive elements by the Curries marked a turn from traditional to modern chemistry. (3)

Both Oxford and Cambridge's curricula reflected the development of scientific chemistry. Cambridge has more than a 300-year history in the discipline, with alchemy being first practiced there in the sixteenth and seventeenth centuries. The shift to traditional chemistry at this institution was marked by the university naming Italian chemist and pharmacist Giovanni F. Vigani as its first professor of chemistry in 1702. Vigani had already been lecturing at Cambridge for 20 years by the time he received this recognition. His lectures were practically driven and focused primarily on the preparation of medical compounds. (4)

Oxford's introduction of chemistry began in 1682 with the creation of the Ashmolean Museum. Elias Ashmole's bequest included the first laboratory built specifically for chemistry because of his interest in alchemy. (5) Chemistry, however, would have to wait almost two hundred years (1860) until it was recognized as a separate discipline with the creation of a small laboratory attached to the Museum of Natural History. (6)

For most of the 19th century, little experimentation or study of chemistry occurred at the universities outside that taught to medical students. (7) Holmes' training in chemistry, then, would have been primarily focused on medical applications, and not surprisingly, he first meets Watson at the chemistry laboratory at St. Bartholomew's Hospital.

Holmes, of course, had his own chemistry equipment, which Watson describes in numerous adventures as sitting on an acid-stained table. Also mentioned along the way are glassware—in particular, a retort used in distillation—a Bunsen burner, a microscope, and other items such as litmus paper. (8)

Holmes' hands were also described as often stained with chemicals. While this might imply that his work was often intense, others suggest his abilities were less than stellar. Isaac Asimov dissected several of Holmes' chemistry references in the Canon and notes that the descriptions of his efforts implied a rather limited knowledge in the area, and rather "blundering." His one major insight involved the devil's foot root, whose effects when ground and burned imitated that of LSD. (9) James O'Brien's review of Asimov's assessment, as well as his examination of Holmes' interest in chemistry, questions Watson's conclusion that Holmes' efforts were "profound." In the end, O'Brien labels them as "eccentric." (10)

Holmes' reputation as a detective is based in part on his ability to apply science and deductive reasoning to solve a case. At the time of his introduction to Watson, he was already on this path as he developed his test for the presence of blood in a stain. While his abilities might not have been as "profound" as Watson suggested, the application of such skills still placed him above those depending on instinct to solve a crime.

---

1. https://www.theguardian.com/ education/ 2002/oct/16/highereducation.science
2. https://www.arvindguptatoys.com/ arvindgupta/asimov-chemistry.pdf
3. https://en.unesco.org/courier /yanvar-mart-2011-g/chemistry-how-it-all-started#:~:text=Four%20thousand%20years%20ago%20the,chemicals%20to%20treat%20eye%20diseases
4. http://pubsapp.acs.org/cen/coverstory/8032/print/8032cambridge.html
5. https://www.academia.edu/8184648/Chemistry_Teaching_at_Oxford_and_Cambridge_Circa_1700
6. https://www.chem.ox.ac.uk/our-history-0#expand-5
7. http://pubsapp.acs.org/cen/coverstory/8032/print/8032cambridge.html
8. Christopher Zordan, "A Fellow who is Working at the Chemical Laboratory," in Dana Richards (ed) *My Scientific Methods*, New York, Baker Street Irregulars, 2022: pp. 67-70.
9. Isaac Asimov, *The Roving Mind*, New York: Prometheus Books, 1997: pp. 127 – 132.
10. James O'Brien, *The Scientific Sherlock Holmes*, Oxford: Oxford University Press, 2013: p. 120.

RIDING THE TUBE

B y the time Holmes and Watson took rooms in 221B, the Baker Street underground station had already been open for almost twenty years. Despite the proximity of one the earliest stations almost at their doorstep, Watson mentions riding the railway in only three adventures. In "The Adventure of the Red-Headed League," they ride it to Aldersgate. The other two mentions occur when a client arrives by underground in "The Adventure of the Beryl Coronet," and Holmes is called to investigate a murder where the corpse is found on its tracks in "The Adventure of the Bruce-Partington Plans."

Prior to its operation in 1863, the London Underground had a rather rocky beginning. While some ideas for subterranean rail lines date back as far as 1837, the first credible proposal appeared in 1845. Charles Pearson suggested a railway powered by air pressure (such as that used in pneumatic tubes—hence, the introduction of the term "tube" to describe the train system). He continued to champion the idea of an underground rail system. He had already successfully spearheaded the creation of the "Thames Tunnel," used for foot traffic under the Thames River. (1) The route and financing, however, created controversy throughout the 1850s, and digging did not begin until 1860. (2) Even after construction began, several scandals plagued the project, including the embezzlement of more than £20 million in today's currency by Leopold Redpath. (3)

Construction on "The Metropolitan Railway" used a "cut and cover" method. Workers dug a trench under or by an existing roadway. Tracks were laid along the trench and the walls were lined with bricks and then covered with a roof. Once completely covered, a new roadway was built over it, and the line was opened to the public in 1863. (4) The 3.75-mile line consisted of seven stops between Paddington (at that time, Bishop's Road) and Farringdon Street. Baker Street was the third stop from Paddington. (5)

The system used steam engines, filling the tunnel with smoke, steam, and sparks, which often sent passengers into coughing fits. One pharmacy even sold a "Metropolitan Mixture" for those affected by the air. The smoke was not only dangerous for the passengers, but also for the conductors, who could not always see through the pollution. Light and air shafts were bored from the surface into the tunnels to address these problems, and gas lights were provided at stations. (6) Grated "blow holes" in the roadways (now covering the underground) also allowed steam and smoke to escape. (7)

Despite such inconveniences, the ability to travel faster than through crowded roadways made it popular enough that more than 9.5 million people used it in the first year alone. The popularity led to extending the line over time to its current 41 miles and 34 stations. (8)

Additional lines were added to the system by various enterprises, the second being what was then known as the "City and South" line. Unlike the "cut and cover" approach, this line was crafted through the same method used for the Thames Tunnel—the tunneling shield. J.H. Greathead modified the design by Marc Isambard Brunel to burrow a circular channel instead of a rectangular one. The device (essentially the same still used today) bored a hole through the earth, allowing for cast-iron reinforcements to be placed along the sides and roof as it did so. (9) This route also used electric trains, cutting down on the pollution within the original line's tunnels. Opened to the public in December 1890, the fare for this line was a flat two-pence for all passengers. (10)

As these lines appeared, some experienced financial difficulties, and soon, all but the Metropolitan Railway were merged into the Underground Group. This merger also introduced the term "underground" and the "roundel" symbol throughout the system. London took control of all the city's transportation services, including the underground, in 1933, and introduced the first diagram of the current stations.

The underground served the city's population in more than transportation. During WWII, the tunnels served as air raid shelters, a storage facility for items from the British Museum, (11) and executive meeting quarters (sometimes housing Prime Minister Winston Churchill) at the unused Down Street station. (12) Other tunnel occupants include about half a million mice and a mosquito species, *Culex pipiens molestus,* introduced into the tunnels during WWII. (13)

While Holmes and Watson's use of the underground occurred only once in the Canon, Holmes had experience riding the tube. In "The Adventure of the Bruce-Partington Plans," Holmes described recalling the train for the Aldgate station was not covered at all points in the West End. While he did not have access to the first 1933 system map, he still had enough knowledge of the underground in his brain attic to determine the series of events leading to poor Arthur Cadogan West's demise.

---

1. https://www.britannica.com/topic/ London-Underground
2. https://londonist.com/2014/11/ five-things-you-didnt-know-about-the-first-underground-line
3. https://www.thehistorypress.co.uk/ articles/ the-history-of-london-s-underground-railway/
4. https://londonist.com/2014/11/ five-things-you-didnt-know-about-the-first-underground-line

5. http://tube-history.uk/ metropolitan-line.php#:~:text=The%20Metropolitan %20line%20opened%20in,day%20and% 20was%20quickly %20extended.

6. https://www.thehistorypress.co.uk/ articles/the-history-of-london-s-underground-railway/

7. Steven Doyle and David Crowder, *Sherlock Holmes for Dummies,* Hoboken, NJ: Wiley Publishing, Inc., 2010, p. 82.

8. http://tube-history.uk/metropolitan-line.php#:~:text=The%20Metropolitan 20line %20opened%20in,day%20and%20was %20quickly %20extended.

9. https://www.britannica.com/technology /tunneling-shield

10. https://www.nycsubway.org/wiki/ Oldest_ London_Tube_Reopened_(City_&_South_ London)_(1925)

11. https://tfl.gov.uk/corporate/about-tfl/culture-and-heritage/londons-transport-a-history/london-underground/a-brief-history-of-the-underground

12. https://www.ltmuseum.co.uk/collections/sto-ries/war/secret-wartime-history-down-street-station

13. https://www.mylondon.news/news/zone-1-news/facts-mice-london-underground-tube-18097665

BATTLE OF THE DETECTIVES

In *A Study in Scarlet*, Watson compares Holmes to Auguste Dupin, Edgar Allen Poe's Parisian detective. Holmes replies the comment is not the compliment it appears because Dupin was not the "analytical phenomenon" portrayed. Holmes' opinion reflects Poe's own after he wrote three stories, despite the detective being a groundbreaking character.

While known for his tales of the macabre, Poe had an analytical bent as well. Before he wrote of Dupin the detective, he penned a series of essays on cryptography and challenged readers to submit their ciphers for him to decode. Rosenheim argues that Dupin and his approach to solving crime reflected Poe's efforts to apply similar logic to the field of criminal investigation. Police departments were still forming, and their methods were often brutal and not always effective. Dupin set the stories in Paris because they had an established police department as well as the Sûreté, for criminal investigation. (1)

The detective appears in three Poe stories: "The Murders in the Rue Morgue," "The Purloined Letter," and "The Mystery of Marie Roget." He also has a companion, never named, who narrates the stories. (2) All three are considered tales of "ratiocination," a term used by Poe to describe the process involved in solving the three crimes. The term relates to reason (or ratio), and computation. (3) This requires establishing relationships between unknown events and motives to solve complex problems through a combination of scientific reasoning and intuition. The focus is on deviations from the normal, anticipation of others' actions, and information that, at first glance, is external to the case. (4)

Such reasoning is referred to as "abductive." Compared to deductive or inductive reasoning, abductive reasoning includes the use of perception of what may appear as random information or observations from a "leap of inference" that creates a pattern. This pattern becomes a "rule" that can be tested. (5) Through the newspaper and police accounts of the crime scene as well as his own visit to the murder victims' apartment, Dupin makes an abductive conclusion. The strength and agility of the perpetrator, as well as an unusual tuft of hair, leads him to announce an orangutan killed the two women. An advertisement in a newspaper leads to the animal's owner.

This use of reasoning reflects an increased interest in the application of the scientific method against superstitions and customs ordering life prior to the 1800s. Fueled by social fears and anxieties, the public had a fascination with the macabre. Scientific advancements and reasoning could be applied to such concerns and provide a more rational explanation of events without relying on superstitions. When Poe wove the macabre and "ratiocination" into a mystery story, he created a new genre—Gothic detective fiction. (6)

Poe, however, abandoned his detective and the genre after the three stories. J.G. Kennedy argues that he recognized such tales as artificial because the writer had developed the mystery and the solution. He went so far as to mock the process in the next story he published, "The Oblong Box." (7)

While Holmes followed much of the same techniques as Dupin, application of abductive reasoning to solve the cases presented to him —some with Gothic characteristics such as vampires—he saw through the pretense just as Poe did. When the author is in control of the mystery, it will follow the author's logic in the end.

———————————

1. Rosenheim, Shawn. "'The King of `Secret Readers'": Edgar Poe, Cryptography, and the Origins of the Detective Story." *ELH* 56, no. 2 (1989): 375–400. https://doi.org/10.2307/2873064.

2. https://www.britannica.com/topic/C-Auguste-Dupin

3. https://www.merriam-webster.com/dictionary/ratiocination

4. https://litchatte.com/2019/06/27/poe-responds-to-concerns-about-rising-crime-in-the-19th-century-and-creates-the-genre-of-detective-fiction/

5. Grimstad, Paul. "C. Auguste Dupin and Charles S. Peirce: An Abductive Affinity." The Edgar Allan Poe Review 6, no. 2 (2005): 22–30.

6. Michelle Miranda "Reasoning through madness: the detective in Gothic crime fiction" Palgrave Communications 3, 17045 (2017).

7. J. Gerald Kennedy, "The Limits of Reason: Poe's Deluded Detective" in *American Literature*, 47, No. 2 (May 1975): 184-96.

Transgressions: Scandal in the Canon*

The threat of scandal appears in almost a quarter of the tales in the Canon. In four of these cases, clients seek Holmes' assistance to avoid exposure of a Victorian norm violation: three involve letters to previous lovers; the fourth, an attempted theft of an item entrusted to a banker. In the other ten, as Holmes solves the mystery, he uncovers evidence that, if revealed, would cause a scandal for someone entangled in the case. In many of these tales, the mere threat of such publicity is enough to force them to do another's bidding (such as paying blackmail or changing a will). That committing murder is considered a better solution than suffering the negative public reaction to such revelations indicates the power certain Victorian social norms carried (and still do) within certain social strata.

While many behaviors may be unacceptable (stealing, for example), not all are scandalous, and even disreputable behavior can be tolerated under certain circumstances. Ari Adut in *On Scandal: Moral Disturbances in Society, Politics, and Art* defines the public experience of scandal as "an event of varying duration that starts with the publicization of a real, apparent, or alleged transgression to a negatively oriented audience . . ." Three basic elements must exist to form a scandal: the transgression, someone to publicize the offense, and a public who cares or is interested in the offense.

The danger of scandal played an important role in maintaining proper Victorian social conduct, and in several of Holmes' cases, was sufficient to force some to break the law themselves—including murder. Understanding what makes a scandal and why avoiding such exposure in Victorian times provides greater depth and understanding of the motivation behind the crimes Sherlock is called in to solve or prevent.

The Elements of Scandal

Transgressions

As Adut notes, the basis for scandal is the violation of some social norm—either a true occurrence or a claimed one that appears true. The norm must be of sufficient significance for exposure of the offense to create a public outcry and cause deep shame, embarrassment, or significant loss to the transgressor. While certain activities or actions might be tolerated if kept private or within a certain subculture, they will not be accepted once brought to the attention of the greater public.

During the Victorian era, the middle class expanded (from 15% in 1837 to 25% in 1901), creating a large portion of the population. Their core values of hard work, sexual morality, and individual responsibility, according to Sally Mitchell in *Daily Life in Victorian England*, actually spread upward into the upper and aristocracy classes, transforming their behavior. For example, while aristocratic extramarital activity was not kept secret, by the 1840s, such behavior was no longer shared openly and by the end of the century would have removed men from their seats in Parliament.

Publicization of the Transgression

According to Adut's theory, common knowledge is not enough to create a scandal. Rather, scandal occurs when the public is informed simultaneously from a single communicator. The higher the status of the communicator, the greater the significance of the deviant behavior shared and the greater the public's negative reaction to this news.

The Victorian era saw a major increase in newspapers and similar publications (broadsheets, pamphlets, etc.) due to a number of factors. At the beginning of the 1800s, taxes on paper, stamps, and other associated items remained high to cover the costs of the war with France, increasing the price of newspapers throughout the 18th century and into the 19th, until they were reduced and then eliminated in 1830. The rise in literacy rates expanded the reading public and the demand for newspapers. Advertising was introduced and expanded to offset the costs of publication. Technology such as railways and telegraphs also improved the speed at which information flowed, generating greater access to current news. This immediacy and widespread dissemination of such events produced the type of publicity needed to construct a scandal.

An Interested Public

A major portion of the public reaction to scandal involves the contamination of those within the transgressor's social group. Those within the strata must strongly and immediately condemn the action to avoid painting all those in their group as committing similar offenses. Given that elites, in particular, are expected to be role models for appropriate behavior, most scandals are associated with this group.

During the Victorian era, noble families (those identified as a Baronet and above) numbered less than 600. Squires, who were at the bottom of those considered part of the aristocracy, were estimated at

2,000. An affront to the norms in this rather small and interconnected group would quickly spread and just as quickly be reacted to. While some activities might be ignored, if they were to reach the greater population, the whole of the elite would be affected. Publicity related to such events would bring swift rejection of both the offense as well as the offender.

Scandal in the Canon

An Overview of the Stories with a Threat of Scandal

The "Scandalous Stories" table provides a summary of the fourteen stories with some aspect of scandal as part of the mystery for which Holmes is consulted. In seven, women are the victims. In all cases, their past comes back to haunt them and threatens to ruin them—unless they do as the possessor of the knowledge tells them. In several cases, written evidence in the form of letters or even a poorly disguised novel will end an engagement or destroy a husband's reputation. In the eight cases where men are the victims, their fear involves tainting their reputation to the point of losing their livelihood.

To understand the control a threat of scandal had over its victims, the broader context of Victorian society and its code of conduct must be understood.

Scandalous Stories

Story	Victim	Instrument of Scandal	Threat	Outcome
The Hound of the Baskervilles	Laura Lyons	Letter	A married woman writing to another man and requesting that they meet at night	When she learns the man who convinced her to write the letter is married as well, she tells the truth.
"A Scandal in Bohemia"	King of Bohemia	Letters and Photo	To be shared with bride prior to the wedding	Irene Adler plans to destroy the King's engagement but finds and marries a better man. Returns letters, but keeps the photograph to keep the King honest
"The Adventure of the Noble Bachelor"	Hatty Doran	Secret marriage and husband (thought dead)	Will be a bigamist if first marriage revealed.	Fakes death to keep second husband from learning truth but is caught and confesses to fiancé and returns to America with first husband
"The Adventure of the Beryl Coronet"	Alexander Holder (banker)	Beryl Coronet (crown jewel) in his possession as collateral is damaged	Damage to a crown jewel will destroy his reputation as a banker	While damaged, the coronet will be repaired—no one will be the wiser
"The Adventure of the Crooked Man"	James Barclay	Reappearance of a Henry Wood (rival suitor) believed dead	True story of events that James Barclay had betrayed Henry Wood during the Indian Mutiny to keep him from courting Nancy (later James' wife)	At the reappearance of Henry Wood during an argument between the Barclays, James dies of apoplexy. Wood's true identity is safe.
"The Adventure of the Empty House"	Colonel Sebastian Moran	Ronald Adair determines the colonel is cheating at cards	If his conduct becomes known, the colonel will be barred from all gentlemen's clubs and lose his source of living	He murders Ronald Adair but is then arrested when he tries to also murder Sherlock Holmes.

Scandalous Stories, Cont. 1

Story	Victim	Instrument of Scandal	Threat	Outcome
"The Adventure of the Dancing Men"	Elsie (Patrick) Cubitt	Abe Slaney knows her true identity; was once engaged to her	Will tell husband Hilton she is the daughter of an American gangster unless she pays him	Hilton Cubitt is shot by Abe Slaney and Elsie attempts suicide
"The Adventure of the Priory School"	Duke of Holdernesse and son (Lord Arthur Saltire)	Kidnapping of Lord Arthur Saltire	James Wilder had kidnapped Lord Arthur to force the Duke of Holdernesse to change his will in Wilder's favor.	James Wilder, illegitimate son, is sent to Australia. The secret is kept safe.
"The Adventure of Charles Augustus Milverton"	Lady Eva	Spritely, imprudent letters written to a "young squire in the country"	Pay a fee for the letters or they will be given to her fiancé (Earl of Devoncourt).	Refuses the lower sum offered by Lady Eva, but prior to Holmes stealing the letters, Milverton is shot by "The Dark Lady"—another of his victims.
"The Adventure of the Three Students"	Hilton Soames, professor in charge of a scholarship program at a university	Stolen Greek exams	Must determine who stole the exam or else the scholarship process will be suspect (loss of honor for the school and the professor).	One student, Gilchrist (son of a Baronet) confesses and leaves for South Africa.
"The Adventure of the Missing Three-Quarter"	Godfrey Staunton	Secret marriage to lower-class woman	Godfrey will be disinherited by rich uncle (Lord Mount-James) if marriage is revealed.	Secret wife dies (natural causes) and marriage remains secret.
"The Adventure of the Second Stain"	Lady Hilda Trelawney Hope, Trelawney Hope (European Secretary)	Letter used to blackmail Lady Hilda to have her steal a political letter from her husband	Trelawney Hope's reputation as government official and the letter, if shared, could cause a war.	Blackmailer is murdered by another of his victims, Lady Hilda's letters are burned, and the diplomatic letter returned without anyone being wiser.

Scandalous Stories, Cont. 2

Story	Victim	Instrument of Scandal	Threat	Outcome
"The Adventure of the Three Gables"	Isadora Klein	Manuscript of a novel	If published, the manuscript would publicize Klein's ill treatment of a young man and ruin her engagement to the Duke of Lomond. Author is dead, but manuscript remains and must be stolen.	Manuscript is burned, marriage saved.
"The Adventure of the Blanched Soldier"	Godfrey Emsworth	Leprosy	Being kept at home, but if discovered, would be sent to an institution, and family marked with the stigma of the disease (incurable at that time).	Turns out to be false leprosy – ichtyosis – and curable.

Victorian Norms and Scandal

In 62 BCE, during a celebration honoring a goddess, Publius Clodius Pulcher, an ambitious politician, sneaked into the all-woman affair with the goal of seducing Pompeia, Caesar's wife. He was caught, and a trial held. Although the women testified against him, Caesar did not condemn him or in any way speak against him. Without Caesar's denunciation, Pulcher was acquitted. At the time, Caesar noted that his wife "ought not even be under suspicion." Any scandal attached to his wife tainted his own political ambitions, and the only course open to him was to sever the relationship. Since that event, women have been held to the standard of "Caesar's wife must be above suspicion."

This criterion was applied in Victorian marriages as part of the notion of the husband and wife uniting "as one." A wife's failure to maintain her moral standing was as much a crime as any legal violation and affected her husband's status as well, as noted by Daniel Pool, *What Jane Austen Ate and What Charles Dickens Knew.*

Sally Mitchell in *Daily Life in Victorian England*, describes women's accepted sphere of influence as the home—a source of peace for the husband and moral upbringing for the children. Thus, marriage defined a woman's "rank, role, duties, social status, place of residence, economic circumstances, and way of life." At the same time, her ability to weigh a future husband's attributes in these areas was limited due to efforts to maintain her innocence before marriage. In some cases, this included any discussion about what would happen on the wedding night.

Men's respectability was based on a resurgence in the concepts of chivalry and honor. As incomes rose and more men could afford the accouterments of the upper classes, gentlemen became recognized by their behavior more so than by their birth. Adherence to the concepts of respectability and honor was to serve as the basis for his actions. Violations of accepted behavior could result in not only the loss of reputation but had true economic impact as well—from the loss of association with business acquaintances, to his job and its income, to loss of marriage prospects for his children.

For the Canon's potential female victims of scandal, evidence that exposed their less-than-pure behavior (a flirtatious letter to a former lover, a father with a criminal background, a secret marriage) was enough to end an engagement (as well as ruin the prospects for any future proposals), end a husband's diplomatic career, or bring about his death. Rather than face revealing their transgressions, they were willing to lie about their role in a murder (Laura Lyons), fake their own murder (Hatty Doran), offer to pay the blackmailer (Elsie Cubitt), commit theft (Isadora Klein and Lady Hilda Trelawney); or hire Holmes to solve their problem, forcing him to commit burglary ("The Adventure of Charles Augustus Milverton").

For the gentlemen, the potential loss of honor lay behind a

continuum of criminal actions, from the theft of a Greek exam ("The Adventure of the Three Students") to an incurable disfiguring disease ("The Adventure of the Blanched Soldier") to attempted murder ("The Adventure of the Crooked Man"). In all cases, disclosure of their actions would have major consequences in their lives, including their source of income (Colonel Sebastian Moran's card games at gentlemen's clubs; Alexander Holder's reputation as a banker; and Godfrey Staunton's and Lord Arthur Saltire's inheritance), being branded a traitor (James Barclay's treatment of Henry Wood), or possible shunning of the whole family (Godfrey Emsworth's apparent leprosy). As a result, they were willing to leave the country (Gilchrist and James Wilder), hide their shame (Godfrey Staunton's secret wife and Godfrey Emsworth's leprosy), die from their shame (James Barclay), or commit murder (Colonel Sebastian Moran).

In such cases, they were seeking to prevent the knowledge they had committed some scandalous act from becoming public. In the publicizing of the transgression, scandal is born.

Publicity

The rise in the number and variety of newspapers also created greater competition—for both readers and advertisers—and led to an explosion of sensationalism, focusing primarily on crimes and upper-class scandals. The papers did not only share the gory or juicy details of these events; the authors and editors would craft them to become "a reassuring set of parables which illustrated [that] virtue [was] rewarded and immorality punished," according to Thomas Boyle in *Black Swine in the Sewers of Hampstead: Beneath the Surface of Victorian Sensationalism*. These stories followed a code of respectability where those who had committed offenses were justly caught and punished—as a lesson to others and a reinforcement of current social values, as shown in "murder in Late Victorian Newspapers: Leading Articles in *The Times* 1885-1905. Sexual deviance cases were also covered, but only hinted at some details to avoid arousing young people and corrupting them to commit acts similar to that of the perpetrator. To highlight the dangers of such actions, final coverage would include the perpetrator's "confession" and a warning to others not to follow his or her bad example.

Beyond any legal consequences of scandalous behavior, the social reaction could be quite even more severe. One of the most well-known cases in this respect is the trial and conviction of Oscar Wilde for homosexual acts. While Wilde's behavior was known and ignored in certain circles, a libel suit spread knowledge of it to the larger population. Legal authorities were forced to prosecute Wilde to reinforce appropriate behavior. After serving his prison sentence, he left for the continent, broken and penniless.

Of the fourteen cases, only two had their circumstances appear in the press: Sir Charles' death in *The Hound of the Baskervilles*, and Hatty Doran's disappearance after her wedding in "The Adventure of the Noble Bachelor." In both these tales, the events related were prior to Holmes' involvement. At the same time, the Canon has its own version of morality tales. For example, in "The Adventure of Charles Augustus Milverton," Milverton recounts how another of his victims, Miss Miles, failed to pay him and her wedding to Colonel Dorking was called off only two days before the event. When Holmes attempts to negotiate Milverton's extortion demands against Lady Eva, the blackmailer goes so far as to threaten to expose Lady Eva publicly to serve as an example to his other victims. A previous victim, however, shoots him, bringing a just end to his tyranny.

An Interested Public

All the cases of scandal in the Canon include at least one aristocrat. The characters range from someone in a royal family ("A Scandal in Bohemia" and "The Beryl Coronet") to squires (landed gentry) in *The Hound of the Baskervilles* and "The Adventure of the Dancing Men."

100

Despite these characters' being part of the rather close-knit social strata, Sherlock Holmes is able to avert or lessen the scandal's potential spread to the greater public in all but one case. To do so, he keeps certain knowledge from the police in six cases: Laura Lyons' role in Sir Charles' death in *The Hound of the Baskervilles*, damage to a portion of the crown jewels in "The Adventure of the Beryl Coronet," the identity of Henry Wood in "The Adventure of the Crooked Man," James Wilder's role in the kidnapping of Lord Arthur Saltire in "The Adventure of the Priory School," the murderess in "The Adventure of Charles Augustus Milverton," and Lady Hilda Trelawney Hope's theft and the murderess in "The Adventure of the Second Stain." He reveals an honorable motive in five cases, resulting in an excused behavior: Irene Adler's efforts to protect her new marriage in "A Scandal in Bohemia," Hatty Doran's secret marriage in "The Adventure of the Noble Bachelor," Elsie Cubitt's suicide attempt in "The Adventure of the Dancing Men," Godfrey Staunton's secret marriage in "The Adventure of the Missing Three-Quarter," and Godfrey Emsworth's disease in "The Adventure of the Blanched Soldier." The course of events eliminates the scandal in two cases: Gilchrist's moving to South Africa in "The Adventure of the Three Students" and Isadora Klein's destruction of the damning manuscript and compensation for the author's mother in "The Adventure of the Three Gables."

Only Colonel Sebastian Moran is arrested and prosecuted. He murdered Ronald Adair to keep his card cheating a secret. Here, the morality tale follows that of Victorian crime reporting: the colonel is not spared either from the law or the subsequent outcomes of his misdeeds.

Agency's Role in Scandal

The basis for the literary concept of agency is power, or the control over one's own life. Scandal shifts the control from the character to his or her social sphere. Once a transgression occurs, anyone aware of the wrongdoing gains power over the offender. In more than one of the cases described here, the one with such knowledge forces the offender to commit a crime they would not have done otherwise—from paying blackmail to theft to murder. They manipulate the transgressor through the fear that their deeds will be shared with the public at large.

Once publicized, agency shifts to society as a whole. Most immediately, the offender's social circle would punish any misconduct with anything from a verbal reprimand to ostracism to full shunning and loss of any form of livelihood. In addition, if the offense is a legal one, the person must suffer a trial where all details will be aired and shared.

The fear of losing one's agency leads many of the victims in Canon to seek to regain power over such information. Some seek Holmes' assistance in doing so, but others take circumstances into their own hands. The morality aspects of these cases, however, make it clear that seeking to regain one's agency can have dire consequences.

* This article originally appeared in R. Haile and T. Bower (eds.) *Villains, Victims, and Violets: Agency and Feminism in the Original Sherlock Holmes Canon*, Irvine, CA: BrownWalker Press, 2019.

INDEX

About Liese Sherwood-Fabre

Liese Sherwood-Fabre knew she was destined to write when she got an A+ in the second grade for her story about Dick, Jane, and Sally's ruined picnic. After obtaining her PhD from Indiana University, she joined the federal government and had the opportunity to work and live internationally for more than fifteen years. After returning to the states, she seriously pursued her writing career. She is currently a member of The Crew of the Barque Lone Star and the Studious Scarlets Society scions and contributes regularly to Sherlockian newsletters across the world.

Her fiction series, *The Early Case Files of Sherlock Holmes,* follows a young Sherlock as he develops into the adept detective the world knows. You can learn about her other books, upcoming releases and other events by joining her newsletter at www.liesesherwood-fabre.com.

Also by Liese Sherwood-Fabre

AN UNCONVENTIONAL HOLMES

THE AUDIOBOOK

Missing boys, an imposter husband, and a bizarre vampyre murder.

Sherlock Holmes ventures into the realm of the unnatural in these three cases: the disappearance of the Baker Street Irregulars, the true identity of a Great War veteran, and a vampyre's grisly death. Crossing into the worlds of the Grimm Brothers and Bram Stoker, he seeks the clues needed to unravel the mysteries confronting him. Can Holmes' conventional methods still function in the unconventional world?

The Adventure of the Murdered Midwife

Case One of the Early Case Files of Sherlock Holmes

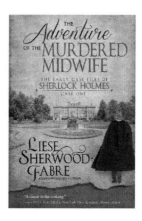

Only Sherlock Holmes can save his mother from the gallows

Violette Holmes has been accused of murdering the village midwife. The dead woman was found in the garden, a pitchfork in the back, after a public argument with Mrs. Holmes. After being called back from Eton because of the scandal surrounding the arrest, Violette tasks Sherlock with collecting the evidence needed to prove her innocence. The village constable will stop at nothing to convict her. Can Sherlock save her from hanging?

The Adventure of the Murdered Midwife
Excerpt

They told me the Battle of Waterloo was won on the playing fields of Eton, and I knew I should have been honored to be at the institution; but at age thirteen, I hated it. The whole bloody place. I remained only because my parents' disappointment would have been too great a disgrace to bear.

My aversion culminated about a month after my arrival when I was forced into a boxing match on the school's verdant side lawn. I had just landed a blow to Charles Fitzsimmons's nose, causing blood to pour from both nostrils, when the boys crowding around us parted. One of the six-form prefects joined us in the circle's center.

After glancing first at Fitzsimmons, he said to me, "Sherlock Holmes, you're wanted in the Head Master's office. Come along."

Even though I'd been at the school only a few weeks, I knew no one was called to the director's office unless something was terribly wrong. I hesitated, blinking at the young man in his stiff collar and black suit. He flapped his arms to mark his impatience at my delay and spun about on his heel, marching toward the college's main building. I gulped, gathered my things, and followed him at a pace that left me puffing to keep up.

I had no idea what caused such a summons. If it had been the fight, surely Charles would have accompanied me. I hadn't experienced any controversies in any of my classes, even with my mathematics instructor. True, earlier in the day I'd corrected him, but surely it made sense to point out his mistake? For the most part, the masters seemed pleased with my answers when they called on me.

I did have problems, however, with most of my classmates— Charles Fitzsimmons was just one example. Except he was the one who'd called me out. Surely, *that* couldn't be the basis of this summons?

Once inside, my sight adjusted slowly to the dark, cool interior, and I could distinguish the stern-faced portraits of past college administrators, masters, and students lining the hallway. As I passed them, I could feel their judgmental stares bearing down on me, and so I focused on the prefect's back, glancing neither right nor left at these long-dead critics. A cold sweat beaded on my upper lip as I felt certain something very grave had occurred, with me at the center of the catastrophe. Reaching the Head Master's office, I found myself unable to work the door's latch, and with an exasperated sigh, the prefect opened it for me and left me to enter on a pair of rather shaky knees.

My agitation deepened when I entered and found the director examining a letter with my father's seal clearly visible. He glanced up from the paper with the same severe expression I'd observed in his predecessors' portraits. Dismissing his appraisal, I concentrated on the details I gathered from the missive in his hand.

Taking a position on an expansive oriental carpet in front of his massive wooden desk, I drew in my breath and asked, "What happened to my mother?"

"How did you know this involves your mother?" he asked, pulling back his chin.

"The letter. That's my father's seal." My words gathered speed as I continued. "It doesn't bear a black border, which means at least at this point no death is involved. My father's hand is steady enough to write, so he must be well, that leaves only some problem with my mother."

The man raised his eyebrows at my response, then glanced at the letter in his hand before tossing it onto the desk's polished surface. "As you have surmised, a problem at home requires your return. Your father has requested that we arrange for you and your things to be sent to the rail station. Your brother will be arriving from Oxford to accompany you the rest of the way."

My heart squeezed in my chest, dread rushing through my body. Home. Underbyrne, the family estate. And not just for a short visit. Packing all my things meant I was leaving for the remainder of the term. Something terribly wrong had happened. Grievous enough to pull Mycroft out of his third year of studies at Oxford. Blood *whooshed* in my ears, and I barely heard what followed.

"I've already requested Mrs. Whittlespoon to assist you in your packing." Head Master turned his attention to the rest of the mail on his desk. He glanced up to add, "She'll be in your room already."

"Thank you, sir. Good day, sir." I recovered enough to respond to his statement, but not to ask the reason behind Father's directive.

With a wave of his hand, I was dismissed before I could inquire. As I closed the door behind me, I heard him mutter, "As much a prig as his brother."

For a moment, I considered opening the door and requesting more information about his assessment as well as what else my father had provided in his letter, but social convention restrained me from questioning an elder—and the Head Master at that. I was left to ponder my unspoken concerns as I returned to my chamber.

By the time I arrived at my room, my trunk had already been brought down from storage, and Mrs. Whittlespoon, the house dame, was placing my belongings in it.

"There you are, dearie." She pointed to a set of clothing on my bed. "You go change into your traveling clothes while I finish this up."

I paused, considering for a moment to ask her what she knew of the events surrounding my departure, but she had turned her attention to the drawer with my undergarments. Having lost the opportunity for the moment, I retrieved the clothes and carried them to the bathing facilities.

Since the Head Master was not forthcoming, and Mrs. Whittlespoon might have only limited knowledge, my best hope for additional information as to what had occurred with Mother would be Mycroft—if he was in the mood to share. Knowing my brother, he might not be inclined to discuss this or any other matter on the journey home. He'd been overjoyed to return to university after the summer's break and pulling him out would definitely sour his mood.

Mrs. Whittlespoon turned to me when I re-entered the room and placed both her hands on my shoulders for a moment to scrutinize my appearance.

"You look a right proper young gentleman." She smoothed out the sleeves of my coat. "You go on down to the carriage, now. I'll finish up here and have Jarvis take the trunk down to the carriage. I assume you'll want to carry *that* yourself."

She waved her hand at my violin case lying on the bed. A wave of guilt swept over me. At my mother's insistence, I'd begun lessons two years before and developed some skill on the instrument. Since entering Eton I hadn't found the time to practice as promised. How could I report such a failure to her? I swallowed as my next thought rose, unbidden. Assuming, of course, she was in a position to ask—or understand—my answer.

No sooner had I taken a seat in the awaiting carriage, resting the violin case on my lap, than a loud clomping at the dormitory door announced the arrival of my trunk. The handyman's back bent low, and he knees splayed outward. The driver helped him take it the final yards to the rear of the carriage with Mrs. Whittlespoon following behind, shouting orders all the way.

"Mind how you secure it. I didn't spend all that time laying things neatly just so—here now, watch that strap."

The vehicle rocked as the trunk was fastened on. When the movement ceased, Mrs. Whittlespoon stuck her head in the window and passed me a small basket. "Something in case you get hungry on the way."

I bobbed my head. "Thank you. It's quite kind of you."

Before either of us could say more, the driver gave a shout, and the house dame stepped back only a second prior to the carriage jerking forward.

Throughout the trip to the station, I turned over in my mind what little I had gleaned from my exchange with the Head Master. I had assumed the issue lay with her health— although I knew her to be quite hale for a woman of forty- six. What other situation would cause my father to pull both his sons out of school? Scandal possibly. Although, she came from a good family with a stalwart reputation, and my mother was by nature a moral upright person. The most shocking character on either side of her parentage was my grand-mother, the sister of Horace Vernet, the artist. Being French and having the patronage of Napoleon III certainly raised eyebrows in some corners, but that would hardly create a scandal worthy of removing Mycroft and myself from school.

The basket Mrs. Whittlespoon had given me bumped my elbow. To distract myself from the thoughts swirling about my head, I took the opportunity to check its contents. A small apple, two thick slices of bread, and a medium wedge of cheese. I found the thought of food unsettling and closed the basket.

Soon after the driver deposited me and my trunk on the station platform, a train pulled in spewing a cloud of smoke and dust. I spotted my brother leaning from the window of a first-class compart-ment at the rear of the train. He pointed to a man pushing a cart toward me, and once free of my baggage, I joined him.

My brother and father were "cut from the same cloth"—as they say—with thick waists and high foreheads. One had only to examine my father to know how Mycroft would appear thirty years hence. The exception being the eyes. Not in color, but in sharpness. My father's lacked the keen intellect apparent in my brother's. While Father was quite an accomplished man—as a squire he served as a justice of the peace and was versed in many subjects, espe- cially entomology—Mycroft's intensity marked him as our progenitor's intellectual superior.

That keenness also gave him little patience with others. Despite being my only sibling, I was never truly comfortable around him. With rare exceptions, I guarded my words and actions carefully in his presence, knowing they would be weighed, and mostly likely found lacking in some aspect. For that reason, when he indicated I should sit in the tufted, blue seat opposite him in the compartment, I didn't argue. He had taken the backward-facing middle seat because it was less prone to the smoke and dust blown in through the window .

I plopped down on the cushion, and a small cloud of ash rose from my action, sending me into a brief coughing fit. When a small smile graced his lips, I ignored it and settled Mrs. Whittlespoon's basket next to me.

Mycroft jutted his chin at it. "What's that?"

"Mrs. Whittlespoon gave it to me. For the trip."

"What'd she give you?"

"You want it? I can't—I'm not hungry."

He took the proffered basket and studied the contents.

Putting the cheese between the two slices of bread, he took a bite and caused my stomach to flip yet again. It hadn't quite settled when the train lurched forward and another wave of nausea swept over me.

To distract myself, I stared out the window at the passing countryside and summoned the nerve to ask him what had occupied me for the past several hours. "What exactly happened to Mother? I know she's not dead, but I have no information beyond that. Is she sick? Dying?"

"She's fine."

"Someone's not, or we wouldn't be called home."

No reply.

"I'm going to find out. Wouldn't it be better for me to learn it from you now, than when we arrive at Underbyrne?"

Through his cheese sandwich, he said, "You want to know, you little twit? Here it is. Mother's in gaol, accused of murder ."

The force with which this pronouncement hit me was the same as if he'd given me a blow to the stomach. The queasiness I'd battled since my fight with Fitzsimmons returned with a vengeance. Bile surged into my throat. The compartment closed around me, and my deepest desire was to flee. I stood, realized there was truly nowhere to go, and dropped back down into my seat.

"Put your head between your legs."

I glanced at Mycroft, but his words sounded as if I were under water.

"Put your head between your legs."

When I remained immobile, he grabbed me by the hair and bent me over.

"Breathe," he said.

After several gulps of air, my hearing improved, and my heartbeat slowed. "You can let go now."

He sat back, and I raised my head. "Mother? Wha— How?"

"I don't know all the particulars. I gleaned it from my own analysis of the information in the papers."

He pulled part of a newspaper out of his breast pocket and passed it to me. Despite the train's movement, my original agitation subsided enough for me to read the dispatch concerning Mrs. Emma Brown having been found dead on our estate.

"Mrs. Brown, the midwife?"

Mycroft nodded. The whole village knew the thin, older woman. She'd been at the delivery of at least half the town. The other half had been seen either by Dr. Farnsworth, the village doctor, or Mr. Harvingsham, the village surgeon. As far as I knew, Mother had little contact with Mrs. Brown. Dr. Farnsworth or Mr. Harvingsham tended us during certain severe illnesses, but my mother relied mostly on her own knowledge of herbs and medicine to treat our ailments.

He then handed me another newspaper sheaf. This one was from a larger paper and included an editorial decrying the bias in some county judicial systems. In point, the author noted a recent incident of a justice of the peace's wife whom a local businessman had accused of his wife's murder and yet the woman still resided at home.

"You believe that this refers to Father?"

"How many dead bodies do you think crop up on the property of justices of the peace? Of course, it's referring to our parents, idiot. And after that editorial appeared, the constable was forced to arrest Mother and put her in gaol."

Calmed by the supplied information instead of my own dire speculations, I returned the two papers to him and contemplated this new turn of events. One didn't argue with Mycroft or his ability to deduce specifics from the barest of details. He had exercised his ability to knit together bits of intelligence from various sources into a whole truth for as long as I'd known him. And he was seldom, if ever, proved wrong.

All the same, one glaring omission remained.

"She's innocent," I said.

"I lack enough information to make that assertion."

Mycroft pulled the apple out of the basket. "You sure you don't want this?"

When I shook my head, he bit into it and then spit out what he had in his mouth. I could see the apple's brown inside from across the compartment. Had the circumstances been different, I might have found this comeuppance amusing. Instead, I found no satisfaction in the event, not being able to shift my focus from the idea of Mother as a murderess. Unable to conceive of her in those terms, I returned to my original contention that she had been unjustly accused. And I had to find out what had truly happened—which only Mother could supply.

At that moment, I resolved to find a way to visit her.

I knew where the gaol was. The old, square building sat on a corner near the edge of the village center. Did one simply knock on the door and ask to see a prisoner, as when calling upon a neighbor?

While I wanted to ask Mycroft about the process, he'd already rested his head back against his seat, his eyes closed. I tried to follow my brother's example but found myself unable to rest. I kept imagining my mother locked in a dank cell and found the only way to keep the vision away was to watch the green countryside pass by my window until dusk fell and all that remained was my own reflection staring back.

Father stood on the station platform when we arrived. He said little in greeting other than, "Simpson's waiting with the cart and the footman. Have them bring your trunks out."

Before either of us could respond, he spun about on his heel and left us to follow him.

Once on the road to Underbyrne, I considered raising the issue of visiting Mother, but knew better than to bring up the discussion in front of a servant. Even one as trusted as our steward, Mr. Simpson. The tall, thin man had been with the Holmes family since before my parents married. Given the lack of safe, conventionally acceptable topics to discuss (somehow the weather and the train ride seemed too mundane in the present situation), we rode the hour to the manor house in silence.

When we pulled up to the front door, the familiarity and *sameness* of Underbyrne held me in my seat for a moment. I saw no change in the red-brick structure with its white-framed gabled dormers on the third floor. Nothing suggested anything out of the ordinary had occurred within. Even the sight of Mrs. Simpson in her usual coffee-brown dress standing stiff-backed under the entrance's covered porch appeared normal.

Only when Father said, "Get a move on," did I stir and retrieve my violin case from beside me on the seat and follow the others inside.

"Welcome home, boys," Mrs. Simpson said. Her strained voice was the first indication of the pall over the house. "Your rooms are ready. Mr. Simpson will bring up your trunks directly. Are you hungry? I had Cook prepare plates of cold meat for you."

I shifted my feet, somehow unable to move farther into the entryway. I glanced about at the all-too-familiar surroundings, seeking some solace in them. In the candlelight, everything had a sort of gilded edge to it, giving off a sense of normalness otherwise lacking in everyone's mood. The entry hall, open to the second floor and lined with three generations of Vernet paintings and the stairway on the right leading to our bedrooms, hadn't changed. Neither had the doors leading to Father's library and office on the right or the parlor and sitting room to the left. The grandfather clock between the two rooms on the left marked the time as it always had.

I glanced at the time. That late was it?

Even the scents of wax and lemon oil said, "home," but I found myself as ill-at-ease as in a stranger's residence.

Ignoring—or perhaps unaware—of my discomfort, Father spoke to me over his shoulder as he passed on to the dining room. "Leave your case in the library before joining us."

Once I was alone with Mrs. Simpson, she held out her hand. "Pass that to me, Master Sherlock. I'll take it up to your room if you wish."

"Is my uncle about?" I asked, handing over the violin.

Her mouth turned down. "He's terribly upset about your mother, you know. He's been keeping to himself for the most part, taking his meals in his workshop. If you like, after you eat, you can take a plate to him. I'm sure he would enjoy a visit from you. Go on now and have a bit of supper. Your moth—" She stopped herself and swallowed hard. "God bless her. She'd want you to keep up your strength, so you could put on the brave face needed at a time like this."

I shifted the weight on my feet. Nothing in the many lessons my father had imparted provided me with the appropriate response for "a time like this." I knew which piece of silver to use with which course, the polite greeting for the different classes of people, and proper dinner conversation; but how did one comport oneself when one's parent faced the possibility of hanging?

Both men were already at the dining table deep in silent contemplation over their meal of cold roast beef and potatoes. I slid into my chair and stared at the thinly sliced meat and potatoes, both with a slight sheen of fat covering them. My earlier repulsion toward food returned, and a lump formed in my throat. Knowing nothing solid would make it past, I sipped the glass of milk beside it.

"Aren't you hungry?" Mycroft asked.

Father lifted his head and studied me for a moment before saying, "You need to keep up your strength, son."

I poked the meat with a fork. Bile threatened my throat again. "What do you suppose Mother is eating?"

He shook his head. "Outside of what we've provided, I suppose whatever they serve her."

"And what's that? Has she told you?"

"I haven't seen her." That statement drew stares from both me and Mycroft. He placed his fork and knife onto his plate before speaking. "It's not that I don't want to. She's forbidden it. The only one she's allowed to see her is Ernest."

"Why our uncle?" Mycroft asked.

I, too, was surprised with her choice. While her younger brother was terribly devoted to her, for all the time I'd known him, he'd actually been more reliant on her than the other way around.

My father merely shrugged. "Her instructions were explicit. I was not to try and visit her, but to send Ernest instead."

"Did she say anything about us?" I asked. "Might I visit her?"

Barely were the words out of my mouth before he responded with a sharp, "No. She said only Ernest."

I wanted to argue, but the firm set of his jaw told me not to pursue the matter further. With a final glance at my uneaten food followed by a churning in my stomach informing me to not even consider sending any of it down, I finished the glass of milk and asked, "May I be excused?"

"You're not going to eat that?" Mycroft asked.

When I shook my head, he pulled my food to his place.

I rose to head to the kitchen.

"Where are you off to?" my father asked.

"Mrs. Simpson asked me to take a plate to Uncle Ernest."

Another shift in the seat. "Very well, but don't stay too long and overtire the man."

In the kitchen, I could see Cook was already preparing a basket for me to carry to my uncle. More of the cold roast beef and potatoes, some bread and butter, and a crock that I was certain contained more milk. Ernest didn't believe in imbibing spirits.

"Finished already?" Cook asked. I nodded. "Good, then. Take this on over to your uncle. I'm sure he'd like to see you." Another bob of the head, and I headed out the back door to the converted barn behind the house. Uncle Ernest had come to live at Underbyrne before I was born. He'd served with the military in Afghanistan, and, as Mother put it, the experience changed him. Tending to keep to himself, he tinkered there on different inventions. For the most part, his devices involved gunpowder and other explosives and new ways of using them to project items toward walls and other objects. More than once, I'd been involved in testing a prototype. Despite several attempts to interest the military in his contraptions, they had never responded to any of his correspondence.

Loud clanging greeted me about halfway through the yard. Whatever he was fashioning involved metal.

The noise masked the arrival of a woman, who startled me as she stepped from the shadows and into my path. Only because her reflexes were quicker than mine did Uncle Ernest's dinner basket not drop to the ground.

"Master Sherlock," she said in a low whisper as she handed it back to me, "I didn't mean to scare you."

"I wasn't frightened. You merely took me by surprise." Now that she was out of the shadows, I recognized her as one of the women who bought my mother's herbs. "Rachel Winston, isn't it?"

A shy smile spread across her face. "How kind of you to remember me."

How could I not? The woman, a maid at Lord Devony's estate, had been married for just over three years and had been coming to see my mother for almost as long. Always for the same thing.

"My mother's not here. Sh-she's—"

"I know. But don't you worry. I don't believe for a minute she had anything to do with Emma Brown's death. Your mother is the kindest, most generous woman I've ever met. The whole village thinks so—at least, them's who know her ."

"Did you want to see my father, then?"

"No, sir. Actually, I was hoping to see you. Do you know what your mother gives me? I'm almost out and..."

Her voice trailed off and both of us glanced toward the greenhouse—my mother's refuge—at the other end of the house.

"I...uh..." How did I explain that while I helped my mother with her plants, the exact nature of their various preparations was not known to me? She had taught me the plants' properties, but I was not privy to the exact proportions or extractions for the concoctions she prepared for "the ladies," as she referred to the village women. "I'm sorry. I don't—"

Her hand flew to her mouth. "Oh, please, sir. I need those seeds. I-I can't have a baby yet." She squeezed her eyes shut and gave a stifled sob behind her hand. "Now with Mrs. Brown gone, the only one left is Mr. Harvingsham, and he won't—"

A sob cut off the rest of her thought. I glanced toward my uncle's workshop and shifted my weight from one foot to the other. Once again, my father's etiquette lessons were failing me. What did one say to a practically hysterical female?

"Please don't cry, Mrs. Winston. I'm hoping to see my mother shortly, and I'll ask her about them. Come back tomorrow night, and I'll let you know if I could determine what she gives you."

She grasped my free hand. "Thank you, sir. Thank you." After turning away from me, she stepped back into the shadows with a whispered, "I'll see you after I get off tomorrow night."

Once she had disappeared, I continued on to my uncle's workshop and knocked on the door. When he didn't respond, I let myself in.

As I stepped inside, Uncle Ernest's shout echoed through the cavernous old barn. "Duck, boy, duck!"

Made in the USA
Middletown, DE
03 June 2023

31732874R00080